CW00448206

Comfortable

Kaspar Zeitgeist

CONTENTS

Part One - Fairly Young

1

'You still don't get it, do you?'

I didn't, quite naturally.

I puffed out my cheeks and sighed simultaneously somehow, staring at her and contemplating, at a snail-like pace, how to respond. It was, it would be fair to say, a wholly rare occurrence that I'd think entirely in tune with her, and that occasion was no aberration from the norm. As I'd freely admit now, which isn't something I'd have done then, I often, quite often in fact, struggled to understand her perspective on many matters. Not for the first or last time, my mind, so unreliable when quick thought would be required, drew a blank on what to say, and, with no words easily accessible, I responded in a non-verbal manner, shrugging my non-gym-frequenting shoulders.

Failing to add anything further to the conversation, I had a post-shrug nod and reassured her that I understood her point of view. Spending an afternoon in Chantelle's company was quite a regular occurrence then, but that moment specifically, that memory, when I think about it now, comes back to me easily, vividly.

I remember her twinkling hazelnut eyes locked to mine with a strength of intensity not befitting the relaxed atmosphere of the quarter-full Islington pub we were frequenting as I conformed willingly, at least outwardly, to her way of thinking. Conformity, always an easy option, has, I'm slightly ashamed to write, been something that has come all too easily to me.

It's not just because it was a bitterly cold March day that the memory of that afternoon sticks in my mind, there have been plenty of those. It's also not because I saw an extremely average Wolverhampton Wanderers side thump Chelsea 4-1 on the television, something less common. No, the fact is, that that day, or more precisely during that very conversation, I felt that rarest of things, something that was at a rather shudder-inducing late point in my life; complete an utter comfort with somebody that I was physically attracted to. My memory of her there, then, that afternoon, is crystal clear, an unfadable picture in my mind. Her jet-black hair was worn up, making her naturally rounded face look thinner, even with her ever-glorious plump cheeks. She was dressed in a fading black leather jacket, which she kept on inside the pub, and she wore a subtle dark eye shadow. Her look was edgy yet classy, elegant yet simple, and she caught the eye of every man and woman in the place. If you'd have told me then, at that exact moment, that I'd only see that girl a handful of times more after that day, I'd have called you crazy.

Oddly uncomfortable silences, dithering, babbling, dobbling, wibbling. They've all been my modus operandi when in social situations. The more nervous I am, the more awkwardness there is. Once, I, in an entirely involuntary manner, started humming in a single dull tone through an attempted conversation with a girl I'd found to be attractive. I was entirely unaware of the fact that I'd been doing so until a friend of mine, who'd been in his own conversation next to us, told me later in the evening. A natural struggler with self-confidence, that didn't exactly give me a shot in the arm going into my next social foray. Indeed, I'd always had, and still do have, a tendency to be terribly uncomfortable around people in a social environment. At least, that is, until I met her. With Chantelle, it felt different. I was consistently being challenged, something which would often have led me to be increasingly introverted, and yet with her I was at ease. I was relaxed yet excited, and crucially I felt confident and comfortable in her presence. I was certain back then that what I was feeling for her, whatever it was - the *great indescribable* I guess - she would be feeling for me too.

I was young, youngish, well, getting on slightly, and by the time I'd met Chantelle I'd been in a few short, sharp, rapid failed relationships. I'd started to see people I knew 'couple-up', friends from school and university, some had even gotten married by then. I was a cynic when it came to marriage, both inwardly and, occasionally, outwardly after a few drinks. I'd have classed myself a realist at the time, perhaps even a modern thinker, but the truth was that I protected myself with that outlook, protected myself from the nagging feeling that it would never be for me, that it could never be for me.

On each and every of the rare occasions when I'd slipped, almost unknowingly, into something that could be termed a relationship, I'd swiftly find myself being judged. Invariably, there was an insistence that I should start making sweeping alterations to my life. They were simple things but I was very resistant to change. 'Walter, you're not very productive are you.' 'Walter you should really do more exercise.' 'Walter, why don't you care about the plight of hedgehogs?' They were all valid critiques, it must be said, and I do care about hedgehogs, but I just dug-in when judgement was passed on me, becoming increasingly set in my ways even at a young, youngish, age.

Chantelle was, is, different in many regards, but I think her willingness to let me be me is one of the reasons that she stood out. She always knew that what makes people unique; their idiosyncrasies, their differing outlooks on life, are usually what make them interesting in the first place. Indeed, I thought it quite possible that it was my failings, my inability to communicate all that well, my vulnerability, and my overly relaxed outlook that she could have been drawn to, as a friend or more.

We were opposites in many ways, not least because she seemed to have a view on almost everything, whereas I've always had a tendency towards ambivalence. And while she wouldn't be afraid to say what she thought, she was, unlike most, myself included, considerate of other peoples' points of view. She'd share her opinion, usually in a highly impassioned manner, strong language accompanied by strong hand gestures, on a range of topics from grand things like the UK's international sale of arms or the difficulties for families supporting their elders, to normal stuff like the technique with which you should make a cup of coffee (milk first apparently), yet while she was strong in her beliefs, I can't recall any occasion, not once, while discussing anything, when she would tell me that I had to think the same, nor did she ever hold my difference of opinion, if I dared to have one, against me. She just liked me to understand what she thought, and why she thought it, and what I did with that, well that was up to me. I liked her for that immensely, instantly, and I'd say I respected her immensely, instantly for that outlook. To express your own point of view and leave the other person to make their mind up is something that very few people did, still do, with most of us choosing to be adversarial either in defence or attack instead. Me, well I wouldn't often get opinionated myself. To her the world was black and white with minute shades of grey; things were simply right or wrong. To me the world was all grey and wholly confusing. Indeed generally, I always tend to think, to feel, that I never know enough about anything to be confident in forcing my views on people around me. I mean, usually when I think I know something about anything, It turns out that I didn't have it close to figured out in the first place.

And so, it was one of those opinionated sorts of conversations that we were having at the bar that day with Chantelle sharing an opinion that 'I didn't get.'

'How could I?' I responded in a defeated manner after that shrug and a large sip of my beer, 'we don't share the same experiences.' The no experiences line was a tried and tested response that I'd used before as a refuge when I wanted to get out of a conversation. Results were mixed. She knew that I was lucky enough to come from a bit of money and it was constantly used against me as a reason that I couldn't understand a certain cause, whatever that might be. There was probably, well certainly, a bit of truth in it and, accordingly, but quite of character, it wound me up. Not many things, if anything actually, managed to rile me up but it was with great resolve that I never outwardly showed my inner frustration in this type of scenario. Indeed, I didn't think my family were rich, and my dear old dad has worked hard in his little shop, back on the island in which I grew up, to put us in a position where we haven't had to worry about finances. I'd gone to a good school and then to university and now had a solid if unspectacular white collar job. She told me that I should appreciate what I have, that being a white man, emphasis on both white and man, meant that I had it easy. I didn't disagree with her, it was impossible to, and yet her talking about it plainly got under my skin.

It's true that I had it easy. I've had very few challenges that have obstructed me from a life of comfort. Indeed, while I've had some challenges in my life, hard times you could even say, I've never had a barrier to financial security. I knew, I've always known, that I hadn't worked hard at all to get to a level of comfort in my life that some people, who worked hard every day, may never get to. I would have probably had to work hard to avoid comfort and security; my straightforward, simple to follow, path of a good school, university, well-paid profession, had been laid out for me so visibly that it would have been difficult to wander off it.

At that time, I had a nice enough one-bedroom flat in a fairly grand Georgian building that I rented up in Clerkenwell. As nice as it was, the flat was in no way special to me and I'd describe it now as a living space rather than a home. It was doubtless only special to the landlord who, through my money and that of every other tenant, earned a substantial sum in return for almost nothing at all. Inheritance. Nevertheless, even after the quite hefty rent, I had enough left over at the end of the month to go to restaurants and bars as I pleased. Bars mainly. That level of ease in my life, comfort, wasn't really of my own making, barely at all perhaps, and I would, somewhat begrudgingly, admit as such to Chantelle. As in this instance, such an admission was rarely enough, and it was said, not in a judgemental way by any means, that I could never truly understand the difficulties of others that I'd never known the likes of. I'd carefully admit to my inherent shortcomings, as I did that day at the bar. Chantelle she was 'probably right,' I'd say, while attempting to maintain an air of nonchalance, choosing my words so as to not entirely concede that she was right, even if I knew she was. Her opinion on most things, through simply having a greater knowledge of them, was probably worth more than mine. That is unless we were talking about accounting, which, quite rightly, we never were.

I've become increasingly stubborn as I've gotten older. I was mid-thirties back then and although, now, I still hold an indifference to most subject matter, particularly political, the type of which used to lead me to silence, I will occasionally throw my own opinion into the mix in a forceful manner. Half the time, I'm not even sure where it comes from and if anybody pressed me for the basis of my 'facts', on whatever matter it may be, it's highly likely I wouldn't be able to respond, at least in a coherent fashion. I'm not really sure why I've grown to do that, 'to lend my two cents,' for any other reason other than a form of self-amusement. As long as I don't run into somebody who actually knows what they're talking about I'm fine, which is something that, with age, I've come to believe is few and far between.

I'm not too clever really, never have been, and that's something I realised quite early in life. I do, however, with a rare sense of pride, consider myself as a reasonably good listener, better than most, and I've been able to learn a few bits and pieces with that listening over the years. That's good enough for me. I'm not winning any prizes for anything intellectual, and I rightly never have, but if somebody asks me something about anything I can draw on what I've heard over the years. Maybe I'm even able to provide some insight into it without having to blindly make something up. Chantelle was impressive, an alien being compared to me, in terms of how she spoke unencumbered about various subjects with such knowledge-powered authority. Her speech would often be frantic due to the high importance that she would prescribe to the subject, whatever subject it may have been. She could often be like an opinion hurricane, destroying weak opinions in her path. It makes me smile when I think back to it. It's not something I have ever had in me, to talk that way, about any topic, and I admired her greatly for it.

If my memory serves me correctly, it was the type of language used by the then government when discussing issues of migration into the UK that was the topic of conversation at the bar that day. I can't remember whether the government was red or blue, but I suppose I wouldn't have really noticed the difference anyway. Would I have any idea about what it's like to be spoken about using derogatory language? Of course not. I was opinionless on the matter, and never could really have been anything else.

Shortly after my concession that I understood that life had been easy for me, Chantelle's boyfriend, yes boyfriend, Thomas, came back from the toilet to re-join us.

Chantelle and I had ceased our discussion when Thomas returned from the toilet, a place he spent an abnormal amount of time. I used to like to think, cruelly and admittedly a bit bitterly, that he had some serious bowel issues. He must have noticed something strange in the air when he rejoined us, as he offered to buy the next round of drinks, something quite out of character, also suggesting that we played a game of pool on the vacant table.

'Pool and beers on me,' he declared.

Thomas and I weren't really friends as such but we'd gone to university together, living in the same halls in the first year, and had bumped into each other at Angel tube station about six months before this pub get together. We'd made eye contact with one another and recognition must have flickered in my eyes, as it did in his, and both of us, powerless against the forces of social etiquette, were forced to stop and talk in the busy station. Our abilities to recognise one another were quite remarkable, each able to negotiate significant changes in our respective appearances with. Both of us were considerably rounder in the face than when we'd last met, whenever that was, possibly a decade earlier. He now had grey hair, a worn face and a minute jet-black tuft of facial hair below his bottom lip which hadn't been there previously, a misjudged attempt to display 'young-at-heartedness' I thought.

We'd gotten chatting in a rushed, slightly awkward, yet pleasant manner, as one tends to do at the station, and one doubly tends to do when you haven't seen or spoken to one another in so long. I'd asked if he was still playing the guitar, 'still strumming the old guitar?' I'd asked, in an inexplicably bizarre manner. It was the sole thing I could remember about him, he responded in the affirmative, and it turned out that he was performing at a pub in the area that evening, and, perhaps seeing only one proper way to continue, suggested that I go along and have a beer with him. To refuse the invite seemed the most instinctive response but with no excuse leaping to the forefront of my mind as to why I couldn't I froze, much like an overweight deer, or hedgehog, caught in the headlights. Rather than rolling into a ball I then said that I'd 'love to' head up there and watch, listen, whatever. Love to, exact words.

In the aftermath of our tube encounter, while I got over the disappointment of being unable to make up an excuse on the spot, I figured that it was only a short walk from my flat, and, actually, why not? It was a Monday evening after all and I hadn't had anything else planned for the night. Against my expectations, as a natural pessimist, or realist perhaps, the evening actually turned out to be a lot of fun and I even suggested we meet up again. It wasn't, however, so that I could see Thomas again.

When something notable in my life has happened, my memory of it, strong and crystallised, is accompanied with whatever, no matter how irrelevant, happened prior to it. I'd just potted the black accidentally to lose a second game of pool when Chantelle nipped off to the toilet.

'Can I tell you something Wally?' Thomas said to me, expressionless, and characteristically monotone.

Wally. I was less than fond of that. Nobody ever called him Tommy.

'Sure, what is it mate?' I said over pronouncing the 't' in mate, but still avoiding an overt declaration of my dislike of the unwanted nickname.

'I've decided I should take the plunge with Chantelle, you know, ask her to marry me,' he said. I was taken aback with disappointment and minor shock, not least because the wording intimated he wasn't thrilled about doing it.

Prior to that conversation, I'd assumed theirs was one of those relationships that wouldn't work out, doomed to fail when Chantelle realised the security of being with Thomas, a fairly wealthy guy, wasn't worth the certain boredom of a life by his side. I still think now that it was a fair assumption to make. While it is true that we, Chantelle and I, had only known one another for around six months, she'd always seemed to me to be a little different, a little less carefree when he was around. The passion in her words and the authority in her opinions dissolved when Thomas, Tommy, was present, as though she was more careful with her words and unwilling, or at least less willing, to say something that he might deem controversial.

Thomas' plan to propose left me a bit woozy, and I think my left eye developed an involuntary twitch. It felt as though somebody was shaking me, slowly, more as if I was on a stationary boat in a sea swell than if I was a piece of ice in a cocktail shaker. Up and down, again and again, slowly, slowly. I never was great on boats, or on cocktails for that matter. I felt sick to my core and it took a moment for me to compose myself. It can't have been very long before I gathered myself but it seemed like an age to me, and I hoped then that the way the news shook me was not too obvious.

When I recall that moment now though, and consider what has happened since, I believe Thomas surely knew that I felt something for Chantelle. Once composed, sort of, I did what everybody does on hearing that news; I said congratulations and smiled, over grinning in a plastic manner. Wholly out of character, I even hugged him to try to cover my true emotions.

'You know Wally,' he pronounced while standing tall, back straight, chest out, 'I've always realised I was a bit lucky, what with having all the advantages in life. Having a bit of money in my family and getting the great education that we did….but this, now, now I've found Chantelle, I truly understand the nature of my privilege.' I shrugged and nodded passively. He asked me to keep it 'just between the two of us for now.'

'Of course, no problem at all,' I said enthusiastically, continuing to struggle with my acting. I asked him if he wanted another pint. I really needed one.

Disappointingly, Chantelle would later say yes to Thomas's proposal. 'Without hesitation.' I was informed by Thomas, oddly, and a year later, they got married in the Kent countryside. She took his last name, in the traditional manner, to become, a touch tongue-twistingly, Chantelle Ellis. I wasn't enthused with what was an absurd name, although some people, strange people or liars, thought it was nice. I focussed my ire on the absurdity of the name but that was, quite obviously, not the cause of my disappointment or anger. I kept my feelings and opinions on the matter to myself, as was my general want, still is, about what I considered to be a mistaken and loveless union.

As a closet romantic, a deeply closeted romantic, it hurt me that Chantelle would choose security and certainty over what it was that we had. Or at least what I thought we had. But I understand that decision, the decision she made then, better now. The past has a rather predictable tendency to inform the present and I've learnt that the people we choose to have in our lives, if indeed we can choose them, the relationships we forge, or choose not to forge, reflect a great deal on what has gone. What we need now is because of what we've had before.

Indeed, Chantelle speaking passionately about the inadequacies of the foster care system on one occasion and her general distaste for unacknowledged privilege could only be informed by personal experience. Perhaps it isn't a surprise that she chose to marry somebody different to me after all. I found out years later, only quite recently in fact, that the reason the wedding wasn't where Chantelle was from, as is tradition, was due to her not having any family. She never told me the ins and outs of what had happened but I gather there was no father in the picture, and her loving mother, who had raised her alone, getting by on cleaning jobs for rich families, had tragically died very young. I never learned the specifics of it, nor did I ask for them, but I believe it was a cancer that was diagnosed too late. I never pressed Chantelle on what happened after her mum's death. If she'd wanted to speak to me about it, she would have done.

As I've gotten older I've come to realise, with a degree of confidence, that there are reasons for the way we are, the way we think about the world, or don't think about the world, that have nothing to do with our genetics. Indeed, I think it's quite sensible to suggest that almost everything we believe in our lives, and the way we are, is determined by our own unique experiences rather than anything pre-determined. To understand somebody's differences in opinion, or outlook, are therefore inherently difficult but to understand that a perspective may be different to mine because of our differing pasts is clear to me, and, although this is something I have come to understand latterly in my life, I believe this is something Chantelle understood from early in her life, mixing with many people who did not share her life experiences.

Although, in the immediate aftermath of finding out about Thomas's intention to propose and the proposal itself I was disappointed and jealous, bordering on angry when thinking of his luck in life. After a year's reflection in the lead up to the wedding, I'd softened, concluding that he was, after all, a nice enough sort of bloke and thoroughly entitled to happiness. That said, it had hurt at the time, the idea of her marrying him, anyone, and for long, dark, periods I'd contemplated telling her the way I'd felt, not that I really had the words. I never had the words. I'd decided that, logically I think, what with me having little certainty of the way she felt about me, it would be ludicrous for me to do so. Self-protective logic for certain but I was right I think. After all, we didn't know each other that well, I mean during much of my twenties there'd been a slice of pizza in my fridge longer than I'd known Chantelle. I'd even bothered to name Ian the Hawaiian pizza. I thought it was funny at the time. And while my instinct told me their marriage wasn't destined for happiness, how did I know? What did I know about any of it really? And, who was I to break them up? Or try to. Time passed, I thought about her less, and the pain diminished. Life went on. I changed for the worse, sure, I lost what small enthusiasm I had for anything, becoming resigned to the very possible reality of a life without love. Our experiences change our character all the time.

2

It was a large wedding; it would have had to have been for me to get the invite. And on the wedding day, having had my own fortune or misfortune to be invited, it became apparent to me that Thomas had been somewhat understating his luck in life as his parent's wealth became clear. The church in which they got married was in the rural village where his parents lived; a quaint, cobble street laden area surrounded with rolling green hills, with the reception in the garden of his parent's house, situated on the outskirts of the village, that was, without embellishment, the most luxurious place I'd ever seen. It was an enormous, palatial building big enough for four or five of my flat to fit inside. It had a large terraced area, on which the reception took place, with a sizable outdoor swimming pool just off it and a jacuzzi housed in a greenhouse that was attached to the main building. Lucky indeed.

There were only a handful of people at the wedding that I recognised from my university days, and I spent much of my time trying to avoid most of them. Indeed, I had no interest in hearing of their successes in life and love, or at least their stories of their successes. Old Harry Brown was there and he was the exception. Harry and I had gotten on well at university, and, although we'd drifted apart, he'd seemingly remained good friends with Thomas. We

4

got chatting and he told me about the mansion house. It had an incredible five bedrooms, three of those en-suite, three separate bathrooms, a games room, a library, yes - a library, two lounges, one which acted as a cinema, and the biggest kitchen that you've ever seen. Most of the fields around the house also belonged to the family, 'not that they bloody needed them,' he said. Too right, Harry. The amount of wealth felt quite intimidating to me with my brain equating wealth to power, and power is scary. I couldn't help but think that Thomas' family wealth must have been, at least to a minor degree, a factor in Chantelle's decision to marry into the family.

The reception was filled with rather uninteresting speeches, notable for the similarity in the type of people making them and their universal overuse of the phrase 'terrific chap,' while the dancefloor, a rather meagrely sized area, was barren and underused for much of the afternoon following the dreary first dance of the married couple. Indeed, my memory of the dance itself is non-existent but I remember it being unremarkable. Uninspired by the first dance, people had stayed away from the shape-cutting area with the dancefloor attendance largely remaining sparse. That is until Harry and I ventured on together in the early evening, our inhibitions entirely lost, drowned in the free drink that we'd been consuming through the afternoon. It is, after all, rather rude not to drink as much as is physically possible if somebody else is paying the bill, especially if you know that that person owns what looked to be about half an entire county. We turned out to be party starters, something I can't often say of myself, and the dance floor then became quite busy. I didn't get the chance to talk to Chantelle on the day but I remember catching her eye when I was doing my thing on the dancefloor. She had smiled and laughed at me and I had smiled and laughed back as she saw me attracting attention from an age-defyingly agile great aunt. I must have looked ridiculous. Oh well.

Chantelle seemed, outwardly at least, to be happy enough on her wedding day, receiving the congratulations of others from what was, by and large, a wedding party made up of Thomas's family and friends. Appropriate to the composition of the guest list there was a general atmosphere of controlled joy for the vast majority of the day, the type of which I have become sigh inducingly accustomed to at upper middle class celebrations. I thought she could have done better than Thomas of course. I mean, it wasn't as though I didn't like him, or thought that he didn't have a lot going for himself, but she was, is, exceptional in comparison to anybody I've ever met. Exceptional even compared to anybody I know of or have merely witnessed from a distance for that matter. She was too good for me, quite naturally, and too good for him too but maybe, in a manner of speaking, she got what she deserved, I mean, in a good way. She grew up not as well off as me for sure and, on that day, seeing that she would have a life of certain security was something that gave me a semblance of satisfaction. Everybody deserves that sort of security in life, a comfortable platform on which you can build as you wish, barely constrained by the barriers that the majority face. I'm certain that that guaranteed ease of life must have been something that was in Chantelle's mind, driving her decision.

Both then, and now, I wish it didn't have to be that way. My heart pounded in my chest as she walked down the aisle, a deep, and quick thudding, echoing from chest to brain. It sounded like regret.

The consumption of booze was unencumbered and constant at the free home bar that afternoon and, the brief and surprisingly successful foray onto the dancefloor aside, the majority of time was spent chatting with Harry Brown. I went into the day with the sole intent of getting rather drunk at the bar alone but, I have to say, doing it with Harry was, arguably I guess, more enjoyable. Turns out, Harry put those university days to pretty good use and became an economic advisor to one of the big banks. I forget which one it was, although it certainly doesn't matter and while, as he himself admitted, it didn't sound a particularly exciting life, he'd created a life for himself wanting for very little.

'It's not particularly glamorous Wally, but beggars can't be choosers and it does pay rather well.'

It was entirely false to suggest that neither one of us had options of what to do with our lives professionally, but with nothing in the way of imagination we'd both chosen the safety of well remunerated dull jobs. Me, well I've been an accountant since university, and with little to no interest in my craft I haven't once been tempted to talk about my job with anybody outside of work, quite rightly. Who cares? Indeed, if I had the displeasure of being in a 'so what do you do?' conversation, I'd often just let the other person in the conversation make the classic joke, and be done with it quickly. You know the one, the one about me being good with a calculator. Big laugh. I'd always laugh as though I hadn't heard it before, or a variation of it, and then the conversation would be able to move onto something more interesting. Easily done. I am, I should mention, quite handy with a complex calculator, but I'd never ever give anybody the satisfaction of fulfilling their joke.

Harry clearly wasn't cut from the same cloth as me regarding work chat. He was willing and comfortable in telling me with unadulterated enthusiasm about the potential impact of different government policies on the banks, and how that could, in turn, even impact on *normal people*. Potentially, maybe. He boldly announced at one point that 'the impacts of policies would not impact different stakeholders equally.' I nodded along as he spoke, as if it was enlightening. The conversation flowed, our tongues lubricated by the free booze, mercifully making those work-related passages pass painlessly. We whittled away hours talking about people we knew in common at university, something that was exponentially more enjoyable than listening about the effects that changes to the base interest rate have on borrowing money. I didn't give as much as him to the conversation myself, but I enjoyed hearing what old what's his face and what's her face were up to in those days. It sounded as though a lot of people had left London and were starting families in nice big houses. 'He's done bloody well for himself too.' Harry would say about somebody that I had a foggy memory of or barely knew. Harry himself had just bought a nice place in Beckenham, not too far from where the wedding was apparently. A bit of a 'doer upper' he said, but I was told that with 'a bit of efficient capital spending' he might just double the value of the property.

'Nice one Hazza,' I said amicably, drunkenly.

Harry was a strange sort of bloke really, in both personality and look, still displaying the same haphazard approach to shaving that he had at university, which continually left a clump of hair around the jaw line of his slimline face. He was full of energy, funny, perhaps without entirely meaning to be, and undoubtedly bright. But despite his obvious smarts it always felt as though he would try to impress upon me that he was clever, as if he were trying to make sure I knew that he was highly intelligent, or, at least, that he was more intelligent than me. It wasn't really something I needed pressed upon me to appreciate. He had a habit of dropping little titbits of Latin into general speech, holding his gaze on me as he would do so, ensuring that I'd noted he'd used an extinct language. Very odd.

'*Ergo*, I decided to opt for the fixed-rate mortgage,' (eye contact held). That sort of thing. I found it a little annoying, but generally, it just amused me. Harry, credit to him I think, was barely unchanged from our university days. Indeed, he was, at the wedding, exactly as I'd remembered him.

'Took one of those home IQ tests the other day,' Harry said as we polished off another free stout each.

'Oh yeah,' I responded.

'Top 2%, *ergo* I could easily be in Mensa,' he proclaimed, standing tall. Ergo was clearly a favourite of his. I'd roll my eyes and say 'right, okay mate' in exactly the same manner as I used to do at university, presuming Mensa was some sort of cult. It felt oddly fantastic, comforting, like going back in time to a fond, carefree, stage in my life. It was as if he were perpetually trying to prove a point to me, and to other people I guess, that he belonged in my company, or perhaps in the echelons of high society. Not that I would be classified as high society mind you.

To me, people sometimes seem to put forward a version of themselves almost entirely derived from a willingness to hide where they come from, whether that be family, education or a certain area perhaps. I'm not entirely sure of Harry's background, but his need to impress could have been an inferiority thing I guess, born from how and where he grew up. There's a tragic obsession with class after all, and he seemed more obsessed than most. Although he spoke as though he was 'well to do,' a way of speaking doesn't always reflect an upbringing but rather an ability and willingness to display a character or persona. For my part, I've always thought that I've just been me but, when I really consider it, even I'm prone to changes of behaviour depending on who I'm around and I can sort of understand Harry's need to fit in. It never crossed my mind to tell him not to focus on where he comes from, or to worry about what other people think but rather that he should be proud of himself for who he is. I should.

In a slightly different way to that in which Harry seemed to alter his persona, one of my good friends from school, Anthony 'Big Tony' Pizzini, also used to try hard to hide his Italian upbringing in order to fit in. Tony's heritage shyness came from the totally unproven 'fact', rumour, that circulated around the school that his family were, quite naturally, Sicilian mobsters. This was of course ludicrous. I think. His family were in Italy and he had, admittedly in quite a strange life decision, moved to the small island I grew up on to ensure he became bilingual. Within about a month of joining the school, Big Tony, so named for neither height nor weight, but rather because of an enormous aquiline nose, had impressively lost his Italian accent and renounced his nationality. It turned out that losing his accent was a darned sight easier than getting rid of his stereotypically wonderful (and very serious) predilection for pizza and spaghetti carbonara. It should be said that it was a rather un-Italian love of Hawaiian pizza that excited him most. That odd penchant actually drew a few of his confused peers into believing that he must have been from the UK. It was Big Tony's drive to fit in, to act normal, which precipitated his altered persona. It was all quite silly, particularly when you consider that being part of a mafia family would have bought him a lot of fear-induced respect.

To give himself increased authenticity as a local Tony would go out of his way to drop, often incorrectly used, British phrases into his speech. The likes of which none of us used anyway. He thought he was the 'Beast's Knees' in doing so. While, towards the end of school Tony dropped the act and embraced his heritage once more, the dodgy British phrases would stay for life. Indeed, as he became more comfortable at school and particularly with certain people he grew to like and trust, it allowed himself to be more natural, his true self, and that was great to see. More than myself, my best friend Sam, who had a real gift for making people feel relaxed, was influential in Tony becoming comfortable in his own skin.

To be able to get others comfortable around you, so much so that they don't feel the need to pretend to be a different version of themselves, is quite a gift to have. I don't think it's a skill I own unfortunately, my awkwardness sometimes even uncomforts myself, oddly. Sam had the enviable ability to put people at ease and Chantelle had it too. She was unashamedly herself in most situations. Quite right too, considering how glorious she was, is, and I think that that authenticity rubbed off on people around her, breathing confidence into them to be their natural version.

To my mind, Chantelle would only ever put forward a modified, controlled, version of herself when Thomas was around. Her swearing, only utilised for descriptive necessity, definitely got taken down a notch for certain. To me there always seemed to be a beautiful chaos surrounding her, as if a fuse was perennially lit, and an explosion of emotion not far away. It made simply being in her presence exciting, and the idea of spending any time together thrilling. I hoped that that fuse would never go out. I always wondered, after she got married to Thomas, who it would be that Chantelle would have those impassioned, opinionated, conversations with. I hoped there would be someone.

They moved out of London, where she'd had most of her friends, in order to be closer to Thomas's family she said, 'making it easier when they were to have a baby.' Spoken as if it was a certainty, despite a tone that intimated Chantelle herself may not have been so sure. And it seemed to me, cynically perhaps, as though baby making was a concession that she'd resigned herself to when they got married. A part of the contract between them, if you will.

3

A number of months after the wedding, I met up with Chantelle back in London. We saw one another for breakfast in a run-down greasy spoon, around Waterloo, that had been one of her favourites when she'd been living in that area. She'd been craving their hash browns apparently. I casually spoke of the wedding, an obvious topic of conversation, which, on being brought up was met with an exhalation that conveyed a fatigue for all things wedding related, quite naturally I guess. I took the cue and didn't bother asking if she had enjoyed it. After commenting with little expression in an odd question style that 'all went smoothly, didn't it?' she perked up when recalling my 'star turn' on the dancefloor. She chuckled to herself using the word 'enthusiastic' to describe my moves. I have to say that 'enthusiastic' is not a word that I often hear associated with myself and I wasn't entirely disappointed with the critique. It was 'all Harry Brown's doing,' I said, lying. Indeed, I'd, quite uncharacteristically, yearned for the dancefloor after a few drinks.

I mentioned what a nice fella Harry was, and told her a bit about him, what he'd told me about his house and job. I accidentally said that he seemed like a 'happy chappy,' not generally an expression I'd use, I guess I was nervous, and that 'a guy like him was entitled to his happiness.' I didn't realise what I'd said

35

could have been so emotive but it was as if a dormant volcano erupted.

'Hmmm, entitlement…' she started. 'Uh-oh', I thought, wincing, with a mix of trepidation and anticipation as for a few expectant seconds I waited for the old Chantelle. She didn't disappoint, letting me know her feelings on the matter and, pleasingly, she didn't quite see it the same way as I did. It wouldn't have felt right if she'd agreed with me. That fuse was perhaps still lit.

Indeed, while I was there thinking, in the rather uncomplicated fashion in which my mind works, that we were all entitled to certain things, it actually turns out, unsurprisingly, that it's not quite as simple as I'd had things down as. 'Entitlement is a tricky one.' I remember Chantelle saying. Damn, I guess I knew deep down it would be. Happiness, for example, is something we are all entitled to, however (there's always a however). 'People can feel entitled to too much and often they do.' She continued to suggest that some people, no names given, 'have an aggrandised sense of their own entitlement.' They, whoever they are or were, 'feel they are more entitled to the big house and the nice life than other people, simply because.' I didn't think Harry was necessarily like that, and I was fairly certain we were no longer talking about him. A big home. I didn't particularly disagree with what she was saying and I decided to just do my usual shrug.

'You're probably right,' I said. Indeed, I continued, 'you are *entitled* to your opinion.' I jested, with an antagonistic wink. I remember thinking that that joke was quite clever for me, which is why I've been able to recall it as I write now. It probably didn't go down all too well but she let it slide, thankfully, and even cracked a smile.

Listening to Chantelle speak, often unable to maintain eye contact with me, I couldn't help but notice a sense of self disappointment as she recognised the hypocrisy of surrounding herself with the same sort of people she was describing so negatively. Those with the superiority driven self-entitlement. If not Thomas himself then perhaps some of his friends, family and colleagues. Fellow golfers maybe. That's unfair; they perhaps have an unjustified reputation for elitism. I'm sure some of them are alright. It made me pretty sad then, and still does now, that she was in and around, surrounded by, those sorts of people. That's not to say they were bad people, but she was of a different mould for certain. She was more rounded, more understanding of others, more worldly you could say, she had a humility that afforded her a different outlook on life and I strongly doubt that she fitted in where she was. I hope that she made her points with them, her feelings known, and stood her ground, giving them hell if they didn't at least try to understand her views. Most importantly, I hope that they, whoever they might have been, anybody really, listened to her when she spoke in the same manner that she would for me, and probably did for them.

After the wedding I rarely met with Chantelle, and only perhaps twice without Thomas present. She never told me as such, but as time passed, as is its tendency, I had gotten the sense that boredom had set in for her. In my experience, observing marriages from a distance well outside the splash-zone, it appears to be natural enough that excitement dwindles while *having* to spend so much time with just one person. It seems to be the way it goes generally. While it would be unfair to suggest that the two of them didn't seem content, they did, speaking comfortably with one another, regaling me with punchline-less anecdotes of house renovations, fixed-rate mortgages, and walks in the countryside. That aside, I felt that Chantelle had pretty quickly, post-marriage, lost the spark that I'd noticed in her when we had first met. Indeed, the energy that I felt almost oozing out of her, on that day in the pub when Thomas told me of his intention to propose, had dissipated. It was a slowness in her movements and a seeming inability to stay in the present as her mind wondered, clearly uninterested in the now, that concerned me.

We, Chantelle, Thomas and I, continued to meet at that same pub in Islington on the odd occasion that they would venture up to London for a weekend. And only when we are alone, Chantelle and I, when Thomas was either in the toilet, playing his guitar, at the bar or talking to other people, would I hear passion in Chantelle's speech. She would seemingly flick on in those moments, and I'd see a glimpse of the girl I'd fallen for. It was never talk about her new life in the countryside that would prompt her old passionate self to emerge but rather a throwaway, baiting comment by me, about the good or the bad in the world, politics, religion. I would even follow the news in order that I could say something contemporary and provocative. Knowing how to draw Chantelle into a conversation is one skill I actually possess. Yes, I consider it to be a skill. I'd just say something like, 'I don't see anything wrong with sending kids to private school,' and then I'd sit back, occasionally dipping in to play devil's advocate if I knew anything on the topic at all. I took great satisfaction in listening to her talk, something I'd have done day and night if circumstances had allowed for it. Bliss.

Thomas, for his part, seemed to be drinking a little more quickly than when we'd all been out together pre-wedding. It was particularly noticeable on one evening in particular, when each time I'd had just a few sips of my pint he'd have vaulted his down his neck and would already be offering to buy the next round. It was certainly not in his nature to offer to buy the drinks, no matter how much land his family owned, so that was baffling in the first instance, and then the frequency, the pace, at which he was doing the drinking was cause for wonder. It should probably have been cause for concern too but the rate of boozing was so swift and impressive it only induced wonder at first. As the amazement subsided, I remember thinking that maybe he was just a little bit nervous about playing his gig that night. There was a young ginger lad gaining a bit of a reputation due to play and the audience was about twice as big as normal. As it was, just before he was about to perform he told me, with a curious sort of grin on his face that I couldn't decipher, with one side of his mouth higher than the other and his half-closed eyes looking through me, that Chantelle was 'up the bloody duff.' Pregnant. She had a 'bun in the cooker' as Big Tony Pizzini used to say.

Thomas had once again decided to tell me important news that I didn't really care for at that pub. I think I've developed some kind of complex with that venue as for a long while afterwards I'd feel as though I was being punched in the stomach whenever I walked past it. I didn't know how to read the situation back then and I'm still not entirely sure now. I couldn't tell whether Thomas was happy or scared, celebrating, or drowning his sorrows. Perhaps, and I thought about this a lot at the time, he was even gloating to me through his drunken grinning. As if being married to Chantelle wasn't enough already he perhaps wanted to let me know he'd fully won, like she was a trophy and having a child meant he could keep it for life.

Indeed, I do think Thomas knew the way I felt about Chantelle, it was probably quite obvious. And if he didn't know then, right in that moment, he would shortly after. That was the last time I saw Thomas and, to be honest, by that point I'd had enough of him, both of them in fact. That may sound callous but, while I enjoyed their company, one of them more than the other certainly, I was deeply jealous of them at that time. It wasn't the depth of relationship they had that I was jealous of, because it seemed quite empty, but that perhaps made it worse. The lack of intimacy and connection in their relationship, at least as I perceived it to be, angered me. I 'didn't have an angry bone in my body,' as my dear old mum would say, but it was torture to see something, someone, being wasted and I was irritated by that. I wished she could have been happier. Perhaps if I'd seen Chantelle and Thomas madly in love, as frustrating as that might have been, at least I could have contented myself with the knowledge that they were a good couple, enjoying life together, and I hadn't been bypassed for nothing. While Thomas was on stage, I decided that something had to be done.

It was one of just two occasions in my life when I've done something entirely, and knowingly, selfish. Although entirely different, both provoke shame in me when I think of them. The other time was when I told the headmaster at secondary school that it was Big Tony that had thrown an ice cream, gelato if you will, on Mr. Hughes' car from the fifth floor of the modern foreign languages building. I felt considerable guilt following the episode, guilt inspired by Tony receiving a full week in detention, so much so that from then onwards I decided to help him out with his use of British phrases. Amazingly, his phrases improved, as did our friendship, and some good, therefore, came from it. The same could not be said of the selfishness of this occasion.

Whenever I think of it now I'm unable to think of anything else for a considerable period, cringing persistently for hours sometimes as my mind obsessed over the detail. Back then, although I didn't know the words I'd use when I was about to do it, I knew it was a bad idea. I'd become desperate. It isn't overly dramatic to say that I would physically ache when I thought about Chantelle, which was constant. It had all become an unhealthy preoccupation. She permeated my dreams, often as an allusive protagonist that I was unable to find, searching until I would be woken by the morning. I couldn't concentrate on anything else; thinking of her took up all of my energy. I wish to god there'd been somebody else I was interested in, somebody neither married nor pregnant would have been preferable, but my mind had become infected. I wanted to be the guy to pop the kettle on for her when she would come back home from work or from picking the kids up from school. Our home.

It barely mattered that I hadn't much seen her in the couple of years previous, that she was a married woman or, indeed, that she was pregnant with another man's child. My brain was scrambled. I'd consciously, purposefully, tried to break this feeling, to snap out of it. There had been the occasional liaison on nights out during that period usually with, I'm embarrassed to say, girls that had at least a vague resemblance to Chantelle. My sense of detachment, combined with my regular cluelessness, seemed to have the effect of actually making me relatively attractive during that period which was a novelty. I think confidence or at least the perception of confidence was achieved when I didn't care about the end result and that seemed to have a positive effect. Being carefree was actually quite a nice change from the stuttering, over-keen, sweat monster that I'd always been. Indeed, it was only when I used to really put my mind and full efforts into it, trying to exude confidence to strangers in bars, that I would seemingly become repulsive to all comers.

So there we were, Chantelle and I, comfortable in a rare silence, as Thomas up on stage doing a sound check. I vividly remember breaking the silence by asking, in an unintended overly amplified voice, if she'd like a drink from the bar. I inexplicably suggested I buy some tequila shots - for probably the first and only time in my life, surprising even myself by my absurdity. She, quite rightly, looked at me as if I was insane. It was only 7pm on a Tuesday evening and she was, of course, pregnant.

'He told you, didn't he?' she said, scrunching up her face to display what had become, by then, an almost perpetual frown that I'd barely seen prior to their wedding.

'Oh, yes, yes he, he did,' I spluttered, physically slapping myself on the forehead in recognition of my lunacy. 'I'm sorry, I forgot, you shouldn't really drink alcohol I suppose, let alone tequila shots!' I said it as though it was a half question, just in case she wanted to bypass the general medical advice and get drunk with me. Bad friend, sure, but the truth was, I could have done with her drinking a little. As irrational as it may seem, I would have been a lot less nervous about what I was planning to do, to say, if I'd known she was a little bit tipsy.

The problem, or at least one of the problems, with not being particularly outspoken or opinionated about too much in life, and not being perceived to care too much about anything, is that when the time does come to say something with a bit of gusto you're really not sure how to go about it. Whenever such an occasion would arise, which was not often, my heart would start thumping at a hundred miles an hour because I knew, or at least I thought, that everybody else would find a passionate outburst so completely out of character they'd take notice. As a man more comfortable with being in the background, people taking notice of me is something I've long been highly keen to avoid. As such, in any such rare instance my anxiety would be elevated to an even greater level than normal.

'Just me then,' I said, scurrying off to the bar, following Chantelle's rejection of my tequila offer, to gather my thoughts and receive some much needed alcohol fuelled courage. What a cliché. The problem I remember then facing was that I quickly played out the scenarios in my mind, in a supercharged manner, as though the fears I had were playing on fast forward, playing repeatedly on a screen at the front of my brain. As I recall it, not once did any of the scenarios finish with a strong positive result. 'Oh well,' I thought, at least I'd prepared myself for the inevitability of failure.

Sadly, it's only a recent discovery on my part that fear of failure, quite natural as it seems to be, is utterly debilitating. As I've gotten older, time passes quicker, or seems to, and as soon as I realised, I mean really realised, that time left is diminishing rather rapidly I've felt regret about the countless times I've held myself back from doing something, or saying something through the fear of it going badly. The moment I'm writing about now is one of those rare occasions when I threw caution to the wind and broke from my general reserved character, unencumbered, largely due to a wonderfully depressing cocktail of alcohol and desperation.

While I was, by my own and others' admission, fairly passive in my youth, with a propensity for procrastination and shoulder shrugging, I believe that this moment, with Chantelle, to be a key contributing factor to the way in which I've conducted myself since, a life stricken with a great malaise and high level of inaction. If there is always some reason, or perhaps a plethora of reasons, events, factors some more important than others, as to why our general behaviour is the way it is, this was, I believe, a defining factor in my personal development. I'd always been towards the thinker and listener side of any thinker, listener, doer, sayer scale, and this tipped me further towards the end of the spectrum, somewhere that I have more or less stayed for the entirety of my life.

I must have looked bizarre to Chantelle as I swayed back from the bar, freshly inebriated to our high table, standing tall and grinning in an attempt to exude extreme confidence. Failing no doubt. She nodded at me as I got back with a thick, dark eyebrow raised. Those thick, sexy eyebrows. I'm an eyebrow man. I clipped my knee on the table as I sat down and swore abruptly in reaction. I regathered myself.

'How are you feeling about the baby then?' I said, quite loudly, struggling inexplicably with volume control again. I was tempted to say 'baby, baby,' but didn't thankfully.

'A little nervous,' she said, cracking a small half smile. I remember thinking that this was my chance, an opening. I thought then that I had only one option. I know now that I had many choices of what to say in response. I should have been a good friend; I should have comforted her and let her know that I would be there for her, for both of them. Instead, I said, with an oddly triumphant tone and a slight smirk,

'Well yes, I would be too in your situation.'

When I write it now, on paper, it doesn't seem the worst thing to say, but the way I said it had backed me into a corner and made Chantelle confrontational. That wasn't something that she needed too great an invitation for, and I should have been more careful with my tone and body language.

'Right,' she said, 'why and what is that then?' Again, options. I had options of how to respond, but my heart was pounding and my brain felt like it does sometimes after heavy exercise when even the simplest of questions can become challenging. The words, so often difficult for me to find in even normal circumstances, were undeniably poorly chosen.

'Well,' I said again, as thoughts of what to say zipped through my brain while I tried to gain a modicum of composure, 'if I was having a baby with a man I didn't love I would be nervous too!' I even smiled as I said it.

My words were careless to say the least, and the way in which they were presented, crude. Chantelle sat there silent, responseless and expressionless, without movement after she'd turned away from me to look at the stage. Although I'd have classed myself as an expert in her body language, I couldn't decipher what thoughts were going through her head, what she was feeling. It was likely to be disappointment in me that she felt, but I hoped that it might have been tinged with a realisation that I was right. For my part, I was immediately downbeat. I knew I'd done wrong, said wrong, and, with my head down, I imagine that I looked similar to a dog wanting forgiveness, a supremely unintelligent dog. She didn't look at me and, in the immediacy of my verbal failings; I didn't want to make eye contact anyway. We continued in silence, no longer comfortable, as she looked at the stage, never turning her head to so much as peek in my direction.

Time was behaving unusually and after a while, it could have been five minutes, could've been an hour, I felt desperately in need of re-initiating eye contact. I'd've liked to have spoken but I had no idea what to say. Why would I have started then? A look, just a glance from Chantelle I thought might have gone some way towards diffusing the situation, of reassuring me I wasn't the worst person on the planet. It wasn't forthcoming and I spent what seemed like an eternity staring at the back of her head. Thomas had started playing on stage at some point during that period of non-communication and had been looking in our direction, even more so than usual. I couldn't for the life of me tell you what songs he'd been playing, something annoyingly upbeat no doubt.

As the mistake induced panic subsided, I was awash with nervous thought and embarrassment, the dark lighting somewhat hiding my sweaty, red complexion. Nobody was looking at me anyway. It was something I'd wanted to say, for certain, but not in that manner, not with those words. At the end of the last song of Thomas' set, Chantelle stood up and finally glanced a look, a stare, towards me. Her skin had become puffy and wet around those huge hazelnut eyes, her look combining disgust and fragility as she seemingly held back a deluge of tears. It was a piercing look that lasted a second, if that, but it will be with me eternally and was all I could see whenever I closed my eyes for a long period after. She got up and walked straight to the exit without looking at me again.

I didn't wait for Thomas to finish his set, what was the point; I'd surely burnt my relationship with both of them. I left the pub shortly afterwards after spending a considerable but entirely incalculable amount of time staring into my pint glass, not thinking, not anything, just staring, my mind entirely vacant, frozen.

The cocktail of shame, embarrassment, and the gut wrenching sensation that came from letting down the person I cared for most in my life tasted so powerful that I felt unable to do anything, to eat, to sleep, to speak, to concentrate. Indeed, in that way, it wasn't entirely unlike an unnamed homemade cocktail I'd chugged down in Eastern Europe in my twenties. It was an idiotic moment with a lengthy hangover, both were. All I ever wanted was for her to be happy, and to cause the pain that I'd seen in her eyes as she glanced at me prior to leaving, to witness that in somebody I loved, and to know that I had caused it, has to be one of the worst feelings I've come across in this life.

Thinking about the pain I'd caused, which was all I could do, caused me great anxiety, not just in the initial aftermath but for a number of months afterwards, perhaps even years. I phoned her several times in the following weeks, only ever receiving one, rather blunt response. Thomas had picked up the phone, purposefully I'd imagined, and when I'd asked to speak to Chantelle, he told me in no uncertain terms that I should stop calling. Neither of them wanted to speak to me, I was informed. 'Neither of us.' He repeated it loudly and slowly to ensure clarity. Very good of him. At least I think he repeated it. The words may have just reverberated around my skull, bullet-like. I apologised, in a hurried, weak, and clunky manner, blaming my idiocy on the fact that I'd had a bit to drink at the time. He didn't respond, opting instead to simply put the phone down. There was some truth in it. No doubt the booze hadn't helped, but it was a coward's excuse and my cowardice only made me feel worse about myself.

Thomas had hung up the phone abruptly, cutting me off when I'd made my poor excuse for an apology. I felt anger towards him at the time. Pretty rude, I remember thinking. In reflection, however, I believe I'd have likely done the same had I been in his shoes. And I've imagined being in his shoes many times, or at least tried to imagine. It's a sad state of affairs when you're imagining yourself being somebody else, who you have almost no basis to admire. Anyway, I gave up on trying to make contact after that and, at that time, I thought it would be the last time I would ever see Chantelle. I spent the evening lying on my lounge floor, on my hideous pea green carpet, staring up at the ceiling, thinking only blank thoughts and entirely numbed by loneliness.

Sometimes it can be hard to live alone, and sometimes it can be harder still to live with other people. I went through a period of dreaming, in both the night and day varieties, that Chantelle would talk to me. That was it, just talk, nothing more, which was the extent of my dreams. I'd wake up with her on my mind and, for a millisecond perhaps, prior to full consciousness, I was unable to tell whether my dream was reality, whether it'd happened or not. I'd then wake fully, feeling alone again, foolish and embarrassed in the wake of my mistake, my mistakes, plural I guess.

At times, during the weeks in the aftermath of our falling out, people would surround me. My friends, colleagues, and family but even then, my tendency was towards a feeling of desolate isolation. A consistent thought, dominating my mood, was that nobody around me, probably wrongly, could get my situation. That they didn't know how I felt; nobody would be able to understand my sense of shame, of self-loathing, of disappointment in the world and disappointment in myself. It was as if I was in a state of perpetual reverie, unable to do anything other than be lost in my own world, my own mind, thinking of everything and nothing. I had hours of blank, vacuous thoughts with no beginning, end or point.

I tried to tell myself in those days, perhaps in a manner that Chantelle herself would have done, that I was one of the lucky ones. I had things others didn't have. Millions of people wished they had half the level of comfort or financial security that I had in my life. What was I complaining about? Every evening I'd go to sleep an optimist, apply this logic, telling myself that I would wake up with a bounce in my step, seeing the good around me, the opportunity in a new day, and yet every morning I'd wake up a pessimist, hating the world I'd woken up in again, and wondering why I should bother getting up. I couldn't shake the nothingness that I felt, the vacancy in my own head, the sense that nothing would really matter so nothing was worth doing. It was all-consuming.

It's strange to me now, when I think about it, and when I write it down. I remember that I wanted to be with people, to surround myself, and yet that desire was overpowered by an uncontrollable instinct that nobody would want to see me. As such, I was, to my detriment I'm sure, unwilling to reach out to anyone at all, unable to let anybody make me feel better, feel myself. At the time, even in my own lostness, I believe I was alert to the absurdity of the contradiction, and yet I was powerless against my own sense that I was worthy of nobody's time.

I'd stopped calling my dear old parents at that time, and even stopped meeting up with my best friend too. Sam didn't notice too much at first. We both tended to be busy enough that we'd only go and grab a drink, or a coffee or something every couple of weeks anyway. It wasn't unheard of that a month or so could slip by without contact. Nevertheless, after a couple of months he gave me a ring and asked if I was 'still alive,' as he put it. Although I was pleased to hear his voice, awash with a strange sense of relief, I lied to him, claiming that I'd been really busy at work and couldn't meet up at the moment. I probably should have come up with a better lie - I'd never been a hard worker. The truth was that I'd been a ghost at work, perennially tired due to little, or poor quality sleep and I'd taken several days off calling in sick during that period, foregoing a day in the office for a day in bed. My hard work lie was easy to decipher, especially for Sam who had always had a canny ability to know when I was lying.

Indeed, Sam's powers of lie detection had been strong ever since about the age of nine when I shattered terrifying old Mr. Guilbert's classroom window. The cricket ball was going to hit the wall, but I'd imparted some of my natural and quite unwanted in-swing on the delivery veering the ball unstoppably into the glass. Under interrogation, four of us were asked what had happened, and we all claimed that it must have been somebody else. From then on, after studying my performance, Sam seemed to know, like a form of human polygraph, when I was lying, even over the phone. There must be something in the intonation or inflection of my voice when I'm a bit creative with the truth that tips him off and sure enough a couple of days after the phone call I found him waiting outside my flat for me when I got home from work. I'd taken to leaving work early without telling anyone in those days, and I was home comfortably before 5pm that day. He was there wearing that beaming smile that he always seemed to have, ear to ear, flaunting his perfect straight teeth.

'I knew you wouldn't be working too hard Walter Dorrian!' He shouted at me as I approached, still about twenty-five metres away from one another and with plenty of bemused people in between.

At first, during those days, I was reluctant to spend time with Sam, especially to let him into my flat, the site of which, when he eventually wrestled his way passed the unwashed clothes, still greasy take-away pizza boxes and empty beer bottles made even Sam a little downbeat. It was not a source of pride. Indeed, my flat was the epicentre of my self-loathing and was truly disgusting, fully reflecting how little I cared for myself, or how I looked. But the thing with Sam was, he didn't judge me, at least outwardly. In fact, he didn't really do anything particularly notable, and that was exactly what I needed at the time. I'm certain he knew I was in a bad way mentally, but he intuitively kept his distance so as not to smother me. He played dumb, pretending, more effectively than I ever could, that he didn't recognise that anything was wrong.

Everyone is probably slightly different, but when I was feeling like that, like nothing mattered, that I could do no right, the last thing I felt as though I wanted was for someone to choke me with love and affection. All I really wanted was to be left alone and yet I still enjoyed having the comforting knowledge that there was somebody there for me, with me. That's what good old Sam did. He didn't force me to do anything, he wasn't all over me, he just let me be and let me know that he would do anything I needed from him, whenever. He made out as though it was casual, not bothering him in the slightest. For anybody else it would have probably been annoying, frustrating, but for Sam, selfless Sam, it was something he seemed to want to do, to ensure the people he cared about were okay.

It certainly wouldn't be too far a stretch to say that I loved Sam. It wasn't the same feeling as I felt for Chantelle certainly, but there was a trust and a loyalty between one another that gave me a sensation that was unique to our relationship. I haven't read nearly enough philosophy or poetry to have a clue about what love is, indeed, I haven't read any philosophy or poetry at all really, but I still think no matter how much I had read I'd still be sceptical about anybody claiming to have some great insight. Unless they were French of course, they could know I guess. We all have our own experiences and therefore our own opinions, but for me, and in no way claiming to be an expert, quite naturally, any relationship that brings about heightened feelings for the wellbeing of that person can be classed as a type of love.

Many nights around that time, Sam'd come by and we'd just sit there watching television, barely talking to each other in favour of comfortable silence. I'm sure it wasn't his idea of a good time and it wasn't mine either truth be told, but there was something about him being there that made me feel better about myself. Somebody was willing to endure spending time with me and that was reassuring for my ego. Nights at home alone would be intolerable but when Sam was there, and although he did nothing special, his presence alone gradually brought me to a better headspace. I say he did nothing special; he had this 'Sam Bang Bang' chicken curry, self-named, that he used to make which was tremendous. Never say yes to extra hot bang-bang.

Figuring out what is right for myself, what will lead to self-improvement, is not something that I've ever been able to master, so to be able to go even further and know what others may need tends to be entirely beyond me. Sam had a gift though, an intuitive understanding of what people required. He was able to size up what I needed, giving me a combination of space and reassurance, and it worked well enough as I slowly began to feel myself. He would often be waiting for me when I'd come home from work with that wide smile dominating his slight frame. God knows how he managed to get the time off work because I wasn't exactly working any overtime during that period. 'Another day, another dollar.' He'd often say in a cheery manner, as I'd approach from the tube stop.

Gradually, over the weeks I'd give a little bit more to the conversations between us. We'd cook together in the evenings and I even got good at replicating the 'Sam Bang Bang' chicken curry. A mild version. Little by little, the self-loathing would diminish.

My relationship with Chantelle, and that somewhat tumultuous time, has undoubtedly been a contributory factor in the person I've become, for both good and bad, and the knock on effect of my mental fragility during that period to the rest of my life has been undeniable. It's a period that I now look back on with great regret. It's easy to say now that I should've moved on quicker, but the depth of despair I felt was great, real, and while what I did now seems more trivial, it seemed as though it was the most important thing in the world at the time. I was so absorbed with my own problems, as small as they were in the grand scheme of things, that, regrettably, I failed to notice that Sam himself was entering into somewhat of a mid-life crisis. That is an understatement.

5

It's hard to remember how friendships start, the graduation from somebody being somebody you know to somebody being a friend. You get some people who say they can pinpoint an exact moment when they knew that they would be friends with a person, friends for life sort of stuff. Something they said, something they did. I'm not entirely sure that can be true, it takes a lot of little moments before I can consider somebody a friend. Time to judge somebody's character, to bond, and anything other than that formula for friendship seems foolish to me. Perhaps other people can be instantly more trusting of others than I. It could be that it is the nature of people from small places or little communities to be wary of people they, we, don't know. It's a guard I guess, something about self-preservation, an inherent sort of conservatism. Folks in London have a tendency towards something similar; they aren't instant friends for life kind of people either - they, however, just seem to be straight up scared of other people as opposed to suspicious. The difference is, that while island folk remain suspicious for longer, in London, if a person realises they don't have to be scared of you, the relief of that seems to induce a strong and quick bond. All I know is that that is the way I am; guarded, sceptical, I take a while to ally with somebody and even with Sam, it was a sequence of small things that made me warm to him.

Sam and I came from the same place, we went to the same school, with Big Tony Pizzini, at which we were inseparable, and, following school, we moved to the UK at the same time, heading off to different universities and then both got jobs in the Capital. We lived together for a couple of years towards the end of our twenties, before Sam decided he wanted to get a place of his own. By then, we'd both found our way into solid employment and the ageing process had started to become visible. My hair had begun to thin ever so slightly and Sam, who I thought would look fifteen forever, had begun to pick up the odd grey hair. It was, when we stopped living together, perhaps time to move on, to move apart, but it felt like the end of an era, a move towards adulthood. Living together had been a lot of fun, easy and dramaless but Sam'd wanted his own space and that was reasonable enough as we pushed into our thirties. We went our separate ways, in terms of living arrangements, but we kept in touch frequently, meeting for drinks, and even playing five-a-side football together weekly.

That seems more than a lifetime ago now; not least because just the thought of running doggedly around a football pitch being shouted at for a lack of effort makes me feel nauseous. The physical shape I've let myself get into is of slight embarrassment to me and I should've tried to never stop playing. At the time, I suspected jealousy might have been a reason for Sam wanting to break up our living arrangement. I was, without being some kind of prolific ladies man, doing okay with the girls back then in my own clueless, bumbling sort of way and while Sam was undoubtedly better looking, cleverer and more sociable than me, he never did seem to start any relationships to speak of. There were always girls around him, friends with him and I dare say they were interested in him in a romantic manner. Girls from university, girls from work, but nothing ever seemed to stick. It was something I found rather perplexing but it was, as close as we were, never a topic we tended to discuss. Indeed, if I ever attempted to broach the subject, which was a rarity, he'd tend to swiftly move us onto chatting about something else.

'Come on, we don't wanna talk about that, do we?' he'd say. I guess not.

It was perhaps strange for such close male friends to rarely speak about girls, or women, particularly back then. Only when we were in a larger 'pack' of male friends would it perhaps come up in conversation and, on those occasions, the subject would certainly be brought up by somebody else. Sam was generally evasive and uninterested in those laddy moments, even when, well especially when, Dirty Mike from my office would ask us enthusiastically to mark barmaids out of ten. He, Mike this is, was always the first to put his hand up for a post-work beer and always reckoned a girl he rated an eight or nine was well within the spectrum of what he could attract. Dirty Mike was full of false confidence and undeniably wrong about this and most things I reckon. Still, seemingly unconcerned about being wrong, he'd love throwing his opinions around, particularly after a couple of lagers. To a certain extent, I admired this type of blasé attitude, unafraid of looking stupid, which he did constantly. At least outwardly, he didn't seem to mind what people thought of him. He was a nice enough bloke I guess, always with an amusing anecdote to hand, but he lacked charisma, and, dare I call the kettle black, intelligence. He was perhaps, related to his intelligence, horrifically chauvinistic. I've actually kept in touch with Mike a bit, strangely, little to do with any effort on my part, and I think he's now on wife number four if I've kept count correctly. Honestly, it could be five or six. I can't imagine he was everybody's cup of tea but we got on okay. Chantelle would have hated him with a passion had they ever met. Indeed, Sam wasn't that keen on him either, often just ignoring him in group conversation.

Even at junior school, Sam had always been popular with everybody, girls, and boys alike without having a girlfriend or seemingly having any interest in having one. He was intelligent, funny, trustworthy, and better looking than me for certain with his curly blonde hair. That infectious and unassuming smile was attractive to all, and as he had with me, he always had a way to know if anybody needed an arm around them, despite us being so young. To know when and how to comfort people might have been something he'd learnt from his parents, but it looked so natural to him. It seemed as though it was an innate quality, something he was born with. I'd like to think that I have that ability, or at least have learned that quality over the years, but I'm not so sure. And if so, I definitely don't have it the way that he did.

It's probably due to my interest in football overpowering any curiosity I've had in politics, history or literature but I'm not sure I've gained much wisdom in my years. And, while I daren't say anybody should necessarily listen to much advice of mine, one thing I have learnt, one thing I'm certain on, is that I should've, and you should, engage with your friends' interests. That is to say, I should have engaged with the interests other than the ones I already shared with my friends. Indeed, on a similar note, choose your friends by their character, not their interests, and then learn about what they enjoy doing. If possible. I was never forceful with Sam about how we should spend our time, what we should do, but we got into a bad routine. Particularly further on in life, we just did the things we'd always done, and they tended to be the things I wanted to do, like going to the pub and watching football. Our relationship stagnated a bit because of it. Good old Sam never said anything against it and I think he was content in the time we spent together and in keeping his things, his interests, for him alone. I always thought, assumed, he was the independent type and derived pleasure by keeping his things to himself but if I knew then what I know now, I would've made an effort, even during the times that I was feeling low myself. I would have made myself do the simple stuff, the things that required little effort but I failed to do enough; to ask him what book he was reading or go with him to the theatre, to learn and engage with him about those things that he adored.

Davies was Sam's surname and that meant, due to alphabetic order being a much celebrated way to order the seating plan in most of our classes at junior school, we would sit close or next to one another. That was how we first got to know each other, by chance really. It was one of the best pieces of luck that ever happened to me I think. In one of our early classes, when we must have been about eight years old, I'd done particularly badly in maths homework and he could see when I got the result back that I was on the verge of tears. I might have grown to be quite relaxed and passive in later years but when I was a young school kid, I wanted to be the best at everything. It wouldn't be until a few years later that I'd understand I wasn't going to naturally be the best in the class, and a few years later again that I would realise that other attributes can be just as important as natural born intelligence.

As the inadequacy of my effort on the homework sunk in, I was welling up inside with embarrassment and disappointment. With tears imminent, on seeing my reaction, a seven or eight year-old Sam grabbed my hand, told me not to worry, and let me know, with absolute certainty, that I would do great next time because he would help me. The tears, or the potential tears subsided, replaced by a gratefulness, surprise and, although I didn't realise it then, a newly born trust. Indeed, while it wasn't a single moment that forged our friendship, indeed, we were already acquainted before that point, it was an act of kindness that I remember to this day, and it was undoubtedly an enormous building block in our relationship.

With more and more of those little blocks, we built our friendship. Indeed, another block that has stayed firm in my increasingly less dependable memory is that of the overnight orienteering trip on the common land in the north of the island at the end of the first year of secondary school. I would never class myself as being overly rebellious at school or a teacher's nightmare, but in a situation like that, where there was scope to, I wasn't shy in flouting the rules. As such, I'd decided that it would likely be amusing if, during the middle of the night, I went and collapsed the tent of one of the older students that was accompanying us as a sort of chaperone, Jimmy Cox. Come to think of it now, it might have been a punishment for him. Cox was meant to be in charge of us and was duly given the authority to dress us down or report us to the teaching staff if we misbehaved. This was a level of authority which he revelled in, thoroughly enjoying his newfound power to make our lives absolutely miserable.

So, on what was a blustery evening, it seemed to me highly attractive to pull out some of the pegs that were holding Cox's tent to the ground. It would have been good to knock him down a peg, so to speak. Unfortunately, due to a characteristic lack of planning combined with an extremely dark night, it was a poorly conceived venture, equally as poorly executed. Needless to say, I ended up sabotaging the wrong tent. Indeed, Mr. Hughes, a notoriously angry PE teacher, was awoken at about 5am with his tent flapping about and collapsed on top of him. Hughes, recognised to be one of the least calm teachers in the school, known widely as 'El Veino' due to his slightly dark Spanish-like complexion and a vein that would protrude from his forehead whenever he was shouting at a student, was not a person to mess with. On realising the mistake I'd made, I fully expected all hell to break loose in the morning. As it was, it wouldn't be until sports day, three days later, which marked the last school day of the year, that Hughes sought his revenge.

Hughes gathered all members of the orienteering group, the older students included, which was excellent, to do laps of the athletics track after sports day had finished until somebody admitted what they'd done on the field trip. I'd won the 400-metre race earlier in the day and had, up until he gathered us around, been in a pretty great mood. I needed to think about what I was going to do and I whispered to Sam, who already knew it was me, quite naturally, to seek his advice while we meandered through our first lap. He suggested that I stood firm. 'For all Hughes knew,' he said, 'it might have been the wind on its own.' As we spoke to one another, unfortunately and unknowingly, David Jensen, one of the biggest and strongest, but least athletic boys in our year group and well known already for pushing people around, had overheard us.

'Either you say what you did or I smash your face in.' I remember Jensen threatening, bluntly, from behind us as he struggled with his breath. It was aimed at both of us. We got back to Hughes after our first lap and with DJ staring me down I was about to admit what I'd done. As I opened my mouth, readying myself mentally for a barrage of shouting and physically for further punishment, Sam put his arm across me and shouted,

'I did it sir, I'm very sorry, I didn't realise it was your tent.' The class was dismissed with Sam to stay behind. I waited for him. He had to do eight laps and twenty-five press-ups following each lap. I don't know why he did what he did but it was the kindness that he showed towards me all through his life. I waited until he had finished his punishment when I hugged his slight, exhausted frame tightly, apologising, and thanking him in equal measure.

Through the rest of our lives, for Sam and I, our friendship was a reinforcement and growth of that that had blossomed at school. Even though I'd say, as far as a clueless sap could ever know, I was in love with Chantelle, I'll likely look back on my life when it's drawing to a close and know that the relationship with Sam was the closest thing I've had to an enduring love. Sam didn't make my insides churn the way Chantelle did. My senses didn't feel heightened like when I was with her, but our relationship, our friendship, was closer, far more intimate than my relationship to Chantelle. The bond between me and Sam was forged by trust, of knowing that the other person had your back and would help you in any situation without question. We were as comfortable in silence as we were in laughter. We had complete trust in one another; we made each other happy and to me that is, at the very least, a low grade of love, if, indeed, you can have gradations of such a thing. And yet, despite our bond, our love, I'm certain now that we should have spoken more of how life was treating us, how we were getting on, how we were feeling.

At secondary school, I'd often copy Sam's subject choices so that we could spend most of our days together, as long as I wasn't forced into a different set, a lower set. One such class that we used to have with each other was philosophy. It was in our fifth year if my memory serves me correctly that we had Mrs. Hill's Thursday afternoon class, sixth period. It was a lethargic type of class generally. Regardless of it being only Thursday the entire class would already be thinking towards the coming weekend and, while we were pretty well behaved, there was never anything achieved in that class. Mrs. Hill, pleasant and intelligent as she was, never succeeded in creating enough energy in the classroom to get us involved. It was a dull, quiet class and the heating always seemed to be on, making it sleep inducingly warm. Indeed, I remember Tony Pizzini falling asleep one afternoon so deeply that he was snoring. Mrs. Hill tapped him on the shoulder without success and had to shake him quite aggressively to get him awake. Tony woke up all flustered.

'Sorry Miss, it's just that I'm absolutely cream-crackered.' Sure, it wasn't an expression anybody ever used but he said it correctly and I felt a great deal of pride in that.

Despite those lessons generally being utterly forgetful, something my exam results attested to, there is one lesson that comes to my mind all these years later.

Sam had become oddly engaged in the subject matter and was even debating with old Mrs. Hill, something entirely unheard of in any of our classes and slightly disconcerting for any students who, like myself, didn't want a new standard to be set. I'm not even sure there was a whole lesson on the topic but the debate was about the ability for a person to entirely own their own mind. I remember thinking that the topic was, like much of that sleepy class, overthought, philosophical nonsense. For me it was simple; of course I owned my own mind, nobody was thinking for me, debate settled. Needless to say, Sam was somewhat more thoughtful on the issue.

Sam was intrigued by the theory that our thoughts, and our resulting actions, were determined by the environment that we lived in. Essentially, so the theory went, we've all been programmed through our upbringing to think in certain ways and our own beliefs therefore, aren't really entirely ours. When Sam spoke in discussion, he did so with an uncharacteristic desperation, an urgency, and perhaps a slight anger.

'But Mrs. Hill,' I recall him saying in a stressed manner, 'do you think it's then possible for somebody to know their own mind, understand their own feelings, and then to disregard them anyway due to the environment they are in?' On hearing his engagement with the subject I remember Mrs. Hill looked to be positively beaming as she thanked him for his question. She then thundered, again uncharacteristically, into a diatribe about our general willingness to 'conform to the norm', and the way that willingness can control our actions if not the entirety of our thought process. Sam was eagerly hunched forward over his table. I'd never seen him like it, he was a great student for certain but normally he was entirely relaxed, seemingly care free. I didn't know what to make of it.

'Is conformity unavoidable?' he asked without putting his hand up.

'Not necessarily,' she said, 'and this is the crux of the debate. The level of conformity, the extent, is likely to be dependent on the environment and, perhaps, the individual.' Sam slumped back into his chair.

Sam talked about it, what determines our thoughts and actions, off and on for days after that lesson. To me, then, the idea that outside forces were affecting my judgments and actions was ludicrous and unthinkable. Maybe my lack of willingness to engage in such a debate was due to an environment where free thought and class engagement weren't popular with my peers or at least perceived to be even in class where debate was promoted. Laziness and detachment was definitely regarded as the cooler option, or at least it seemed to me to be regarded as the cooler option. I'm not so sure now.

I've always known that Sam was clever but my appreciation of his intelligence has certainly increased as I've gotten older. He had an enviable ability to process information quickly, to seemingly debate that information with himself, and to then draw his own conclusions. Of all people, he'd have probably been the least susceptible to mindlessly accepting any old information, or instruction, or group thought that would have altered his opinions or behaviour. At the time, sadly, I had a tendency to ignore him when there was something intellectual up for discussion. I'd often choose to bring the quality of the conversation down to my level by switching the subject to something that required lower intellect. It's a point of regret now. I would often choose to disengage with anything I had little understanding of, not attempting to learn or try to understand, opting instead to ignore it through fear of seeming stupid rather than make any attempt at personal growth.

'Even if you can own your own mind, which you probably can't, what's the point if you can't apply what you think in your own life anyway?' I remember Sam saying one night when we'd decided to go camping on the common land near to both our houses on the island. We must have been around fourteen or fifteen and had managed to get hold of a couple of cans of beer. For me the booze slowed down any tendency towards inquisitiveness but it did the exact reverse for him. The 1 am question talking was rhetorical thankfully as there's no way I could keep up with him. Mind you, he wouldn't have expected anything like insightful answers from me as I slipped in and out of consciousness.

'What if we were all allowed and able to think independently and then to act upon those thoughts as we saw fit, free from judgement?' Sam and Chantelle would undoubtedly have gotten on famously. I think that lesson, those questions, that despair, may have been something that I'd have forgotten about in time but Sam would, from time to time, speak in a similar, frantic, manner years later when we were living together in London. Again, often after a beer or two.

'Walter, do you think we are prisoners in our own minds if we cannot act in a manner that follows what we truly think?' he would say.

'I'm not really sure,' I would respond in my non-committal, unengaged way. He would use me as a sounding board, knowing fully well that I would provide little response. I should have tried harder to respond.

'The problem is Walter, society creates limitations on our own range of thought, and even if some of us can press beyond that, and it's a big if, and our mind can go beyond the boundaries that are placed upon it, we cannot act upon it anyway through fear of being different.'

'I think this might be beyond my boundaries of thought,' I said, jokingly. To which he responded that he wished neither of us had any boundaries. He smiled his big smile, holding his gaze upon me and I smiled back. I had no idea what we were smiling about. It was a strange moment and I've forever held on to that memory. It has come to the forefront of my mind since what happened, happened.

Much like myself, Big Tony was not one for deep thinking. It was the summer after we were in Mrs. Hill's philosophy class that he graduated from being somewhat of a peculiar outsider to being a school legend. He wasn't a peculiar outsider to me it must be said. We had grown into quite good friends and we'd often head off to the beach together, him, Sam, and I. Indeed, Tony became well known throughout the school and, I imagine, was known to future students in a legendary capacity once we'd left school. Tony's legend was forged when he survived what was known as the Great Summer Science Block Disaster, for which he was, sheerly by coincidence, the only person in the building, and, quite improbably, entirely unable to explain what had happened. Given that Tony was in the building to redo his regular term chemistry coursework, due to an inadequate first attempt, it's perhaps not surprising that he was unable to explain why the building had combusted.

There was no evidence discovered to indicate how the fire had started and, as such, nothing to suggest that Tony may have started it himself accidentally or otherwise but his well-known fondness of pyrotechnics and a dislike for that building certainly raised questions in my mind. If I had to guess, and I have to because I never asked him and he never told me, I'd say he set fire to something accidentally and then claimed ignorance. I thought he would tell me what happened when he felt ready but he never did. Regardless of what Tony's role in the fire was, it was a story that created gossip, myth and an instant legend. Everybody thought he did it on purpose. Rumours of how and why spread, rumours that he didn't go out of the way to dispel. I heard that he thought the teacher who had failed his coursework was in the building and he was trying to take care of him, mafia style. That was a particularly prominent rumour. He was no longer Big Tony and he embraced his new, more agreeable, nickname, Firestarter.

The legend that was created gave him this unmistakably menacing aura to any kids new to the school and from time to time, we'd stand outside the school gates flicking a Zippo lighter open and closed, grinning, just to amuse ourselves. I wouldn't say it was popularity exactly that Tony gained but rather a form of notoriety, and it gave him the impetus to become more relaxed and comfortable in being himself. Indeed, he began to talk more openly about his family and his joy at going back to Italy during the summers. Home. He even said he didn't care about being an outsider anymore. He was going to 'throw all tits to the wind' and be himself. I physically slapped my forehead after hearing that one. I had, and still have, no idea what he meant.

It was great that old 'Firestarter' found the confidence to be himself after a couple of years. I'm not sure what Sam made of Tony's attempts to fit in and also to then be true to himself with regards to conformity. I don't think Tony would have ever thought about how his environment was changing him, but he worried about being treated like an alien by his peers and he altered his behaviour, quite naturally I guess. Sam never treated Tony like an alien and, as he did with me, had the ability to make Tony comfortable in his own skin even prior to the Great Summer Science Block Disaster.

6

Sam instinctively knew from a very early age whether I needed space, or to talk, or to laugh, or to have some fun on the occasions when I was feeling down. His powers for empathy have stood out to me, perhaps due to it being such a rare quality in a world where people struggle to understand one another's perspectives. After a while, I'd begun to forget about my problems with Chantelle and life began to get back to a degree of normality with far fewer mornings spent paralysed in bed unable to muster the courage to face the day. Low ebbs became less frequent due to him and the time and help he gave me through that period was the nicest, most selfless, thing anybody has ever done for me. I'll forever be grateful.

Overall, it took me months to get back to being a semblance of the person I had been and, sure, some days I relapsed into not wanting to get out of bed and on many occasions I still couldn't face going to work and putting on a false face for the day but, without Sam, I'm certain it would have spiralled into something a lot worse and I'll forever be grateful for his friendship, his powers of understanding, and his commitment to helping me. It was, regretfully, a period of my life during which I had become unable to focus on anybody but myself, and while I did so, I missed something, something important. I couldn't tell, or I didn't realise to be more accurate, that Sam, behind his perennial smile, was himself feeling helpless.

As I returned to being myself, or a mental state that felt more like it used to, when I could get up and face the day without an overload of distress and self-loathing, I started to see Sam less frequently. We'd just meet up to go for a drink once a month or so, if that. He would often tell me that things had gotten busy at work, that we were due a catch-up, and would apologise for not seeing me more often. We were both getting middle-aged by then and we'd drifted apart slightly as our increasingly experienced heads sometimes got more responsibility and consequently more hours at work. The joys of unintentionally entering into middle management. Indeed, I'd started to get asked for opinions on things like 'processes for moving forward' and 'optimal methods for performance review' by senior management figures. Needless to say I offered very little in the way of opinion, and that seemed to be exactly what was required. I was an unashamed yes man, not necessarily because I didn't have the backbone to share an opinion or say no but because I didn't care enough to say it. Through just time passing, I even got a little team to manage, and my complete lack of leadership management skills or knowledge didn't seem to get in my way. While my team performed very averagely, according to the efficiency review system I'd participated in setting-up, they had a good level of camaraderie, and even enjoyment, which I saw as a veritable success.

It was true that Sam too was working a bit more I could tell, and whenever we'd meet up he'd be visibly on the tired side, his boyish looks struggling to fight off the deepening bags under his eyes, even if he was able to maintain his regular good-form, cracking jokes and reminding me of times past. Despite spending less time together than in previous years, I never had the feeling during that period, three years, or so, that he was anything other than happy. Time was passing by for both of us though, earning money, being content, but not really doing anything, nothing interesting, nothing memorable. It was easy, easy to fall into that life of comfortable nothingness, perhaps I even wanted it, but I wonder now about the things that could have been different, what the alternative choices were, and what was my contribution to the way things ultimately turned out?

Sam went home one autumn weekend to the island to see his family, something he did fairly frequently, always bringing back a local cheese that would remind me of home. This visit was different though. Sam went for a walk along the cliff paths alone on a blustery, drizzly, grey day to the south of the island and halfway round, at one of the highest points, he jumped off onto the rocks below, at the point where the land became consumed by the choppy sea, plummeting around thirty metres to his instant death.

I received the news through an 8am phone call from Sam's grief stricken mother, Pamela, the day after it had happened. Dear old Pam had always been softly spoken but I could barely hear her choked up voice on the other end of the line that day. And while I've heard it be said that, for some, when a person hears news of tragedy the words are forever ingrained in their memory, but for me the stress had a different effect as the shock caused me to become so flustered that I can't remember Pam's words. All I remember is my physical reaction, of instantaneous numbness, and then the inadequate words I myself responded with,

'I'm so, so sorry - thanks for letting me know.' That's all I said, and I remember saying it over and over again, repeating it frantically with no sense of calmness or stoicism. In my mind, the conversation lasted minutes on end, but I think it more likely that it would've been a mere thirty seconds. The truth is I don't know, it's blurry. I sat on the cold tiled floor of my kitchen unable to move, no tears, no nothing, before dragging myself to bed mid morning. I'd never experienced loss before and as much as I've told myself that death is inevitable, that it's going to happen to me and everybody around me, when it happened, suddenly, it created an unavoidable shock.

At that point in my life, I don't think I'd cried or even thought about crying since I was about seven years old, possibly that day when Sam calmed me down after receiving that bad maths homework result. How inane. For me, initially, I was completely unable to process the what and why, as if I couldn't understand the sentence that I'd been told. It made no sense to me. And then, when I finally realised what had happened, it released something, like a dam breaking. I wept uncontrollably all night, unencumbered by the regular reflex to suck it up, born out of the understanding that men don't cry. I spent hours solely thinking of my loss until I was drained of all my energy, lying lifeless and immovable on my bed, above the covers, so alone.

I'm not entirely sure how I did, but I managed, improbably, to organise my thoughts sufficiently so that I got myself on a plane to the island the next morning. I recall a zombie-like, weak, weary figure looking back at me when I peered into the mirror of the airport toilets just prior to boarding. When I was physically able to summon the strength to feel and to think once again, it was an overriding sense of guilt that predominated my feelings, a guilt that has been a constant sensation in my conscience ever since. I have always considered how my own lack of resolve, the degree of my own self-obsession, had contributed to my inability to see what was going on with Sam. And how did my own unwillingness to talk about the things that mattered to him, anything meaningful, lead him to think that his only option was to do what he did. To kill himself. My problems, or rather my problem, that had been all consuming for so long and had directly impacted on Sam's life, became so trivial in an instant. Was it my fault? I could have done things differently. What if I'd just shaken off my issues with Chantelle quicker? What if I'd met up more with him in the last few months and years? What if I'd engaged with him more in his philosophical musings? What if I'd let him know that I cared about him? Was I too absent a friend?

The funeral was a typical affair I guess. People were wearing their black attire, going to a church for the first time since their last wedding or funeral and tears from one person spread like a contagion to the rest of the congregation. I was asked to speak and I felt compelled to do so. I got up and said some wholly inadequate words, quite naturally, that in no way came close to expressing how fantastic a person Sam was. My embarrassment and nervousness when speaking in front of people, that had persisted through my life, even in front of small groups, wasn't present. I couldn't muster the strength to care, to worry, to be anxious. I used to hate it at funerals, still do, perhaps even more so now, when people speak specifically of what the person did in their life, almost going through a checklist of achievements. The truth is that for almost one hundred percent of people their achievements on paper are rather underwhelming. Instead, I decided to speak of how Sam made me feel, how he improved my life. There is no way that my words truly reflected my feelings but they seemed to chime with the people at the funeral as the whole collectively sobbed over their loss. I spoke from the heart, possibly for the first time in my life, of the joy and happiness that he brought me when we would have fun together, from our days at school to the last time I'd seen him a couple of weeks earlier. I spoke of his ability to change my mood from anxious to relaxed through his presence alone. I spoke of the warmth that I felt towards him when he would help me in any times of difficulty, however small or large, and I spoke briefly, but I think, candidly, with my voice cracking, about the way in which I felt I'd let him down, my failure to notice his pain.

Dear old Pam, resolute to ageing, barely looking a day over fifty, came to me after the service, tissue in hand and with rare dark bags under her bright blue eyes. Even with her mascara running down her face, induced by unavoidable tears, she'd managed to maintain an air of class in her grief, owing to her calmness and her willingness to ensure that others were getting on okay. She thanked me for my words and told me of how much Sam had loved me. She loved me as well, she said.

'Whatever you do Walter,' she finished by saying, 'we must try not to, in any way, blame ourselves for what happened to Sam. That would be of little use whatsoever, to anybody, and it simply would not be true.' I had that all too familiar pain in my throat that came when I felt like crying but did everything to not. It was reassuring to hear, but as comforting as her words were, I'll always believe that had my actions been different I could've saved Sam from the way he must have felt in those dark times. If only I'd been there for him, the way he was *always* there for me. In a pointlessly stoic manner, I held back my would-be tears after she spoke. We hugged with a long, warm embrace in which I think we were both pretending we were holding Sam. As we said our goodbyes, she gave me a sealed envelope with my name on it that Sam had left in his bedroom the morning that he'd died.

I couldn't open the envelope straight away; I didn't know what to do with it. I was staying with my parent's in their spare bedroom, wiling away the days, doing nothing except to feel sorry for myself, basking in the feeling of comfort and safety that staying with them gave me. Finally, after a week spent staring out of my window at the wind and rain and contemplating what the letter might say, I decided that it was time to open it. I remember, even after I'd made the decision to open it, I hesitated when I took the envelope out of the drawer of my bedside table. I

85

took a deep breath, opened it slowly, my hands even trembled as I prepared to read it.

Dearest Walter, The inability for me to live out the life that I have always wanted has driven me to depths of despair that I never knew to be possible. I have been, for forever it seems, in an ongoing battle with myself and my surroundings. At times I have tried to fight myself, to suppress the person that I know I am, while at other times I have yearned for the world around me to change, to accept me so that I may accept myself. To be perennially caught between the person you are expected to be and the person you want to be is, and has been, an intolerable position. I would not wish such a thing upon anybody. We must be true to ourselves and we must be allowed to be true to ourselves; we must always own our thoughts and actions.

You, Walter, have always been more than a friend to me; you have been my one true love. My last wish is that you mourn little for my passing and fill the rest of your life surrounding yourself with the ones you love. Isolation, physical and mental, has been my life-long enemy and is one that I hope you are able to avoid. Life without freedom is not worth living. Live free my only love. Yours eternally, Sam.

Part 2 - Not Young Anymore

7

Following the funeral, my intention had been to go back to London but Sam's death stirred something in me; a willingness to remain in familiar surroundings. The island, to me, has always seemed like a safe harbour, free from many the pressures, stresses and busyness of normal life, the regular day-to-day that I wanted to withdraw from and forget. It provides a sanctuary of sorts, a place where I can feel safe and secure. Sam's advice was to surround myself with those that I love and, having spent far too little time in the years prior with my parents without being entirely neglectful, I decided to stay on the island to be closer to them. On some level too, it has made me feel as though I was able to remain closer to Sam with the places that I'd see regularly drawing memories of him from when we were kids. And while, especially at first, that caused a painful reaction, as time has gone by I've come to find that anything triggering such thoughts, of us together, provide me with a sense of warmth and comfort.

As I write this now, it is over three, long seeming decades since I lived on the island as a youngster and, I have to say, it gives me great pleasure to report that very little has changed. It is still the relaxed, quiet place that I remember and while I found it a touch too quiet earlier in my life, the lifestyle that it affords me now is far preferable to the hustle and bustle of a large town or city.

In the immediate aftermath of Sam's death, I hadn't thought it to have had that great an effect on me, at least in terms of the decisions I was making but recently I've come to realise that it perhaps had a far deeper impact than I'd originally thought. My decision to stay on the island for example, which I'd convinced myself at the time was one I'd been thinking about for a while, was one that hadn't really crossed my mind at all previously. It was a knee-jerk reaction and although I thought it to be a brave decision at the time, to leave my life in London, it was actually quite a cautious decision born out of a willingness to withdraw from my normal life. I have, ever since Sam's death, become increasingly less willing to try new things, anything really, instead opting for comfort in the familiar. Indeed, I've felt absolutely no inclination to leave the island to see anywhere new, as have I felt no inclination whatsoever to try a new activity or meet new people of my own volition.

There is a nice old-fashioned pub near to the little cottage I live in which I go to regularly and I've become familiar with the staff and a few of the regulars. From time to time new people will stop in for a pint or two and that little contact, with those I don't recognise, has become more than enough new social contact for me. I've even become more conservative in my eating, and while I've never had an extensive repertoire of food that I cook or been overly adventurous in my choices when eating out, now, perhaps even more so that at any time in my life, I have a tendency to keep my food choices regular, opting almost always for one of three dishes; either fish and chips, occasionally accompanied by mushy peas, lasagne at the pub, or a roast dinner that I eat with my parents every Sunday. The standard of those roasts, once tremendously high, has been in a sad decline in recent months and weeks as my dear old mum has started to lose her memory.

The first time it was noticeable mum was struggling was when on a particularly dreary and eye wateringly cold, late winter's day when she was making a Sunday roast, a roast chicken. She'd always liked things salty and often she'd make the gravy from scratch with an abnormal amount of salt; something I'd gotten used to from an early age and had grown to quite like. On this occasion though, even for her salty standards, the gravy, of which I had put lashings all over my potatoes, was, to me at least, inedible. We had all had a laugh at the time, finding the mistake thoroughly amusing and I felt compelled to bring up the incident in conversation to tease my mum, lovelingly, over the few days after. It was, so we thought, a one-off. These things can happen. My dear old dad, who has always enjoyed a thick coating of gravy and had doused it all over his potatoes prior to taking a bite, soldiered on through the saltiness eating every last morsel, so as to make my mum feel less self-conscious of her mistake. I gave him a literal pat on the back for his stoic endeavours before I left that evening.

'The things we do for love.' he responded with a twinkle in his eye.

While that incident had been amusing, a worrying pattern of memory fades similar to the salt roast started to become more regular with my dear old mum developing an almost daily knack for accidentally putting three teaspoons of sugar in a cup of tea, forgetting she'd already put one in, or two. The memory loss, which currently seems to be confined to short-term forgetfulness, is something that my dear old dad and I are coming to terms with. As quick as we have been to notice that there are issues with her memory we've been equally as slow to come to realise that this is likely to be the start of a one-way road for her, for us. It sounds like it should be a simple realisation, to understand that this likely won't get better and yet the idea that she will not overcome what is wrong with her has taken a lot of time to process fully.

Being on the island to help out my dad through this time has been good for the both of us and I'm glad to have been here. While it's been hard on us to see mum's mental deterioration, something that has further provoked thoughts in me about the shortness of life, I haven't seemed able to muster the same emotional range that I had prior to Sam's death. Indeed, while I don't think that I've ever been prone to great changes of mood, of late, I've felt particularly numb. I've never been a neurotic type, stressing if in disorder, or getting annoyed when the bus is more than a minute late. Sure, some things would bother me a little perhaps; an old flatmate for example, who never cleaned his dishes leaving them unwashed for days, but now, even that, I'm not sure would register with me as cause for annoyance.

Perhaps it is perspective, the realisation that none of that stuff matters. Perhaps the part of me that cared about anything died with Sam. I'm not sure. The truth is, it's probably not even about caring, or being angry or annoyed, or feeling anything. It's that I barely take notice of what's going on around me due to a lack of interest in anything. There's nothing that could stir a reaction in me because I seem to choose to be unaware of it, if I'm even choosing. And yet, while I have this general sense of apathy towards everything, certain, often quite small things can really affect me. A clear sunset or, as happened recently, a family of ducks together at the bottom of my garden have brought me to, or close to tears. I saw my dad kissing my mum on the forehead a few days ago, as he's done hundreds of times in front of me, and I had to leave the room to compose myself. I told my dad that I'd had something in my eye when he looked at me strangely on re-entering the kitchen. I am either overwhelmed by thoughts of love, life and death or completely numb to my surroundings, as though I'm wholly unable to react to anything properly anymore, dislodged from an old normality, feeling everything or nothing. I'm not sure which one is worse.

8

At the time of writing, the island has been my home again for the past six years, and, I have to say, going against the expectations of my young self, I've not become bored of the peace that I've found here, or re-found, in the quiet and slow lifestyle. To be able to see my dear old parents regularly has given me a sense of relief, somewhat appeasing the guilt that I've previously felt for spending years on end away from them. I've been lucky enough to find some well-paid accountancy work that I can do from my own home, requiring little to no effort on my part, and life, as it has tended to be for me, is fairly easy. Older and more weathered, it's straightforward for me to see the advantages with which I grew up, the good schools, easy affluence, no crime and a life devoid of discrimination, which Chantelle would have let me know was a privilege, my privilege. Indeed, the ease of life now is far beyond that which I had in London, which was itself a life more comfortable than most could ever hope for, and more than I deserved.

To witness my parents together, in their loving, long-standing marriage, and considering my upbringing compared to that of Chantelle and that of many has only made me further appreciate my own luck in life; to be a loved child in a stable family. Their success as a couple is particularly notable to me now as I enter an age well beyond when it is too late to develop a long-term relationship. Their life together seems remarkable to the marriage cynicist that I have become compared to how normal I perceived it to be when I was growing up.

I've always had the knowledge that the island is my safe haven, a blanket of security; an easy base camp to fall back to if the adventure fails. My parents, the island, have provided me with the constant comfort of knowing I'd have someone to catch me, somewhere soft to land should I inevitably fall, and this privilege to withdraw from the difficulties of life is one I have now gladly taken with a sigh of relief.

Since my return, I've seen people who I'd long drifted away from and fallen out of contact with. I've had the pleasure, for the most part, of seeing old school friends again, people I'd forgotten about in my haste to do whatever it is I've been doing. One such old friend, Hannah Martin, blonde haired and blue eyed, who I hadn't seen for at least twenty years, was at Sam's funeral. I hadn't thought about her for many years but when I did, it triggered memories of our time together as school kids. I'm not sure I'd describe what Hannah and I had as a relationship, whether it would meet that lofty threshold, but we had briefly seen each other regularly with some kissing involved in the last year of school when, in the final year, the boys from the only boy's school and the girls from the only girl's school on the island took some classes together.

I remember that most of the boys acted as if it was the greatest thing on Earth when we were able to integrate *fully* with the girls. Indeed, there was lots of talk about who was going to do what with who, whatever that 'what' was, and asking each other crudely who we were 'going to go for' became common. But the thing was, we were so unused to girls, so entirely unprepared, that we were all too nervous and unable, unskilled perhaps, to forge a proper conversation, let alone anything more. There were of course the odd exceptions, dear old Sam being one of those who had a natural propensity for being incredibly smooth and easy to talk to regardless of sex. I was really rather jealous of that, at the time at least. Still maybe. Uncoincidentally, but lost on me at the time quite naturally, was that Sam was not part of any of the misogyny. For my part, I was as entirely clueless as always, perhaps even more so than anybody else, and I've pretty much remained so ever since.

I think prior to the merging of the boys and girls at school I'd thought that I would be quite the smooth operator, a charmer, the guy that other guys wanted to be and that all girls wanted to be with. I recall contemplating buying a leather jacket prior to the integration as well as optimistically sourcing a large box of condoms from a rather odd bloke in the school year above me. I think he winked at me during the transaction although he may have just had a nervous twitch. My perceived need for that transaction due to my smooth guy persona was, unfortunately, delusional, youthful, wishful, non-evidence based thinking only, and instead I was a sweaty, bumbling, socially inept boy.

It mustn't have been until around two months into the lower sixth term that I noticed Hannah staring at me. Until then, I can't say I'd really noticed her at all. It was economics class, in a room that smelled like cheese and onion crisps that she'd begun to quite frequently look in my general direction, if not exactly at me, chatting inaudibly to the girl that sat next to her, Rebekka Edwards, while doing so. Every few minutes they'd giggle in unison, in a synchronised sort of way that may or may not have been purposely coordinated. Clueless as ever, thinking very little of it, I remember assuming after one of the classes that I must've had something I'd eaten at lunch stuck on my chin or something. I didn't consider that this was an act that could possibly signify an attraction towards me. What did I know, what have I ever known.

After one late spring economics lesson, I was walking alone through a wooded pathway that led to a road which joined the two schools together, when somebody pushed me into a hedge. For the sake of adding detail, I've since learnt due to a new found dad led appreciation for gardening, that it was an orange firethorn hedge, or bush. This act of shoving a fellow student into some shrubbery was a pointless but fairly common thing for the boys to do, more for the sake of amusement rather than bullying, and nobody would ever get badly hurt. Without hesitating, because if you ever hesitated three or four other boys could possibly pile in and start hitting you, all in good jest, I swung my elbow behind me in self-defence and caught the assailant in the face. I turned around to see poor old Hannah, blonde hair everywhere, holding her face. Her shock subsided quickly to a realisation of what'd happened, and that realisation turned swiftly to tears. I froze, quite naturally, not knowing what to do, I'd just hit a girl after all, something frowned upon in general society. The tears aside, she did take the blow rather well, staying on her feet with ease. Had she chosen retaliation instead of crying she may well have beaten me up?

'Crap, crap, crap, I'm so sorry,' I remember saying after thawing from my frozen state. I went to comfort Hannah, to put my arm around her, and she pushed me away, quite rightly.

'What the hell were you doing?' she exclaimed. I had nothing.

'I'm sorry,' I repeated in response, grimacing as I looked at her. 'What were you doing?' I then asked as politely and softly as possible. Unbeknown to me, we'd 'shared a moment' in economics class and, subsequently, she'd decided to take me by surprise and passionately kiss me in the bushes. Bloody hell, I thought, how forward.

'Crap,' I said once more, exemplifying my ability to choose the right words in the moment, a trait that would be long lasting, lifelong. I apologised profusely again and pleaded for Hannah's forgiveness on account of it being a common occurrence that people would get thrown into bushes and attacked quite often.

'You're all idiots,' she said snappily. No argument from me. Mercifully, her tears abated and with a small smile she then admitted that, with hindsight, it might have been a good idea for her own attack to be frontal. I laughed when she said that, somewhat hysterically actually, trying to make her feel better perhaps. Hannah laughed back and smiled, thankfully, possibly thinking I was a touch insane, and, just like that, even as her cheek began to swell and bruise, I'd been forgiven for cracking her in the face with my elbow.

As surprising as that incident itself had been the fact that Hannah and I then got together to 'hang out' after the same class the next week was perhaps even more surprising. We continued to meet the week after that, and then onwards, after every economics class for half a term, we'd meet up chatting and kissing. That was my first venture into the world of relationships, albeit it would be one that was ultimately short-lived. Sure enough, after that half a term she got bored of me and moved onto someone different. I didn't mind at all really. My experience with girls had begun and I was quite thrilled to have got off the mark so to speak. Indeed, I can't say that I was ever particularly enthused by our liaison or particularly enamoured by Hannah, she was alright. It was the novelty of the experience that I enjoyed and the reassuring feeling that somebody could like me in that way, that perhaps I wasn't destined to be alone all my life.

Hannah and I met for coffee a few weeks after Sam's funeral and I brought up my memory of our bush elbow encounter early in conversation. At the funeral, we'd not spoken of anything more than our mutual grief and our willingness to meet up again. The amusing memory of that episode was a nice way to break the ice. She laughed with the same reserved giggle that I remembered and spoke of her embarrassment as to how forward she had been.

'I could have used some of that confidence later in life,' she joked, accompanying the statement with a shorter, more nervous laugh. I'm unsure as to why she wouldn't be confident as an adult, but I didn't feel it was my place to probe. It might have just been a flippant, throwaway remark, something to be disarming and display modesty rather than anything more notable. Indeed, she was switched on, engaging, thoughtful and while she wasn't by any means an ugly teenager, now, if she had a lack of confidence it was unlikely to be due to the way she looked. Her skin, which had had a good coat of acne at school, was unrecognisably unblemished, and her teeth, in braces at school, were about as perfect as you could imagine. In stark contrast to myself, she was practically glowing when I saw her at the cafe, healthy and vibrant. My skin has become notably more pasty in recent years, almost a bone white, increasingly lifeless by the hour, while my hair, not to be too detailed, has been diminishing.

Hannah's husband was, and still is, a local politician, one of the ones that 'actually does something,' she told me, as if it was something that she was programmed to say when speaking about him. She has two grown up children, an older one, a girl who works in the City of London and a younger son who was doing a medical degree at University College London. Dare I say it, the lack of confidence remark aside, she seemed content in life, happy even, unable to contain her white smile as she spoke of her family and her general fondness for island life.

I couldn't help but look at her life, the stability of the partnership she was in, the children she'd had, the happy family she's made, and wonder what could have been. Not necessarily to have that with her, it must be said, I'm not sure we were overly compatible, but to have what she had, with somebody on the island. It all seemed so easy, so simple, and even easier than my life had been. That said she did seem to only be interested in her children and while our conversation had been reasonably engaging, we did spend a lot of time discussing them, well, she spent a lot of time discussing their 'achievements' and I listened. It wasn't my idea of good conversation, and I even tried to, wholly out of character, and unsuccessfully, turn the conversation towards local politics. It was nonsense that they were introducing paid parking in the town centre, wasn't it? I didn't care and I don't think she did either. Back on to the kids.

It's something rarely far from my mind these days, the question of whether that was something I've wanted, the wife, the kids. Generally, I've concluded that it isn't and now, I guess, as the stubble on my chin becomes irreversibly grey, that it's perhaps not even really a question I have to answer any more. 'That shit has sailed,' as Tony Pizzini used to say. Even when I pined over Chantelle for so long and boy did I pine, I was so all consumed with the idea of *having her* that I never really contemplated what it would have meant to actually have her. Fifty or sixty years maybe, growing old with the same person and children perhaps, who knows? I guess I'll never know now whether that life would have suited me or not. It could have been nice. Indeed, it sure would be pleasant to share that bottle of wine at the end of the day. Kind of pleasant, we could have a bottle each.

Then again, having known the pain that losing my best friend has caused me I'm not sure how I would ever have coped with losing a wife or a son or daughter, and the knowledge of the possibility of that pain. Knowing how deeply that can affect me has made me question the merits of getting that close emotionally with anybody. Would it be worth it?

9

With no intention of going back to the UK, I thought it likely that I'd never see Chantelle again and although she would make an occasional often anxiety inducing visit to my thoughts, those visits had become increasingly rare from around two years after our last encounter. But then, having largely vacated my thoughts and with me having no expectations of ever seeing her again, she tracked me down and turned up on my doorstep about nine months after Sam's death. She'd heard that I'd left London from Harry Brown. Old Harry Brown! That man, he's so much more than just a guy that can estimate the impact of VAT changes on revenue to the Exchequer. I had, still have, no idea how he knew where I was, but he did, somewhat concerningly, and he'd spoken about me with Chantelle a couple of months earlier when at a dinner party hosted by Thomas. Well, Thomas and Chantelle. Dinner parties, to the struggling conversationalist that I am, are something torturous, and despite a personal preference to see them removed from existence, I'm incredibly glad that that particular one happened.

It'd been eight long years more or less since Chantelle and I had seen one another and, without so much as a message in that time, it was a considerable shock to see her standing at my front door. My excitement, shock perhaps, was instantaneous and so strong that my heart raced, pounding in what seemed an infrequent rhythm. My face felt hot and an excessive amount of sweat, even for the profuse sweater that I am, seeped through my skin from places I didn't know had sweat glands and onto my clothing, a tatty baby blue polo shirt and long out of shape, overly loose, jeans, unfit for the occasion. My exercise regime had been, and continues to be, nothing to speak of since my return to the island; a couple of short sea swims a week during less than half the year, usually involving cold induced hyperventilation and less than ten strokes of breast stroke before retreating out from the water. And while there are schools of thought promoting the idea that exposure to cold water is good for your health, I could feel the years of neglect as Chantelle stood at the door curiously and I stood in the doorway with body-wide paralysis and a rapidly beating heart.

I dare say Chantelle's regime, or a lack thereof, was similar to mine as middle age and parental responsibilities took their natural impact on her physically. Indeed, had it not been for those instantly recognisable eyes, I, for all my time spent thinking about her, would have struggled to recognise her, not least because she'd dyed her hair to become a much lighter colour. While I'd been residually fit from plenty of exercise as a youngster, that had started to desert me a few years before this encounter, and I could tell, in the way that those ever-piercing eyes studied me when I opened the door that she was taken aback by my scrawny arms and sizable stomach, my round face and my deep frown lines. Damn. Indeed, there had become a bit more of me in all parts of my body, except for hair on my head, sadly, and I was unwillingly starting to accept that my best days were behind me.

'Hi Walter,' Chantelle said in an upbeat fashion, with a genuine, wide-smile that caused her cheeks to inflate just like they had always done. I'm not sure if I was physically open-mouthed but her appearance there definitely left my mouth open in my mind. Stunned. It is a curious thing when you meet somebody after a long period of time that you once felt so strongly about. The blood was whirring around my brain and I completely drew a blank as to what the right words were to fit the occasion. Indeed, my panic and inability to formulate the right thing to say reminded me, unfondly, of our last encounter all those years ago. I dare say that she couldn't find words to match the occasion either, and, in the way she was unable to make eye contact with me, I could see that she was nervous, perhaps as nervous as I was. 'Hi Walter' was perhaps a common greeting but this wasn't a common meeting, at least not to me.

'Wow,' I remember responding, wholly inadequately, and followed by a lingering silence as I stared at her awkwardly, not blinking and immediately losing any ability to be nonchalant.

'Chantelle, hi, hello, Jesus, what are you doing here, I mean, I mean, how are you here, why are you here?' I flapped about following the silence.

'I can't just visit an old friend?' She said, pulling off nonchalance in a far more convincing way than I did, or ever could.

'Of course, absolutely, absolutely, come in, please.' I stuttered, as I ushered her into the house and out to a slightly dirty white plastic table and chairs I had, still have, in the little south facing, half-gravel, half grass, suntrap of a garden. 'Shall I put the kettle on?'

'Absolutely, yes please.' She responded politely, smiling at me with her full cheeks beaming again. I gained a slight level of composure as the familiarity of me going into the kitchen and flicking the kettle on allowed me some ease with the situation.

While I have a tendency to forget the finer details, I remember it clearly being a bright spring day, mid morning when she arrived. The weather was fit for the occasion with the garden full of blooming white and purple tulips smelling fresh after a short and sharp deluge of overnight rain.

As I was making the tea, brewed extra long for Chantelle, I decided that I had to approach the elephant in the room.

'I'm surprised that you'd even want to come and see me, you know, after we left it how we did,' I said, after we'd taken the first sips of what were actually slightly under brewed cups of tea. Oh dear.

'Oh Walter, you haven't changed at all, have you?' She responded laughing, but with a half pained expression. I was perplexed by the response, having no idea what she was talking about, quite naturally. 'You were always clueless when it came to women, weren't you?' I shrugged my old, familiar shrug in response to the rhetorical question, and, I have to say, it felt great. 'The reason I was so angry, you see,' she continued, 'was that I knew there was some truth in your words. There was something between us, wasn't there?' She paused and sighed before continuing. 'And, it was something I wanted to deny; I guess in many ways I still do.' I was taken aback, characteristically speechless. A strange sensation of satisfaction washed over me when I heard her words. 'I've wanted to tell you for years.' she carried on. I didn't know what to do, I think I closed my eyes, bowed my head slightly, and ran my fingers through what little hair was on the top of my head. I had spent weeks, months, stewing over the idea that the person I loved was angry at me, disappointed in me, and years thinking of how I'd mishandled things, how I'd affected my own opportunities for personal happiness, how I'd lost a friend. 'I'm sorry.' She said with her wide, honest, hazelnut eyes staring me down, consuming my reactions, my thoughts, my looks.

The conversation flowed from there; I even had the newly found confidence to enquire, jokingly, if she wanted a tequila shot as I did that last night in the pub. She raised an eyebrow and smirked. Now relaxed, we chatted as we used to. My mind, my whole self in fact felt as though it had been transported back in time. It was as though I'd taken a big breath of fresh air for the first time in nearly a decade with my body becoming charged, feeling as alive as it had done all those years earlier. It was the way she used to make me feel. I was enjoying myself, not in some kind of secure nothing to worry about fashion, but in a happy, let's take on the world manner. Well, maybe not quite, but something stirred in me to make me feel as though I could do things. I could even look forward perhaps.

We both became more relaxed and Chantelle proceeded to tell me of her journey to the island. She'd decided to take the ferry instead of the plane because she'd never been on a passenger ferry, citing that it was a rare opportunity for her to try new things, 'however mundane it might seem.' I nodded in agreement, even if my own outlook to trying new things was, or at least had been entirely different in recent years. Indeed, it had been the comfort of the known, the regular that I'd sought of late and the idea of doing something new had long become unappealing. She told me that she had regretted her 'adventurous' decision about a half hour into the journey when she realised that it was very unlikely that she'd be able to complete the crossing without the smoked salmon and cream cheese bagel eaten prior to boarding the vessel making its own return journey.

With an awareness of her fragile state, she'd gone to stand in the outside area and, despite her state of readiness, had proceeded to embarrassingly projectile vomit over the shoulder of a man who she'd struck up conversation with and catching him with what appeared to be a chunk of dill covered salmon on the way. The man, in understandable disbelief and entirely unable to re-engage with any sort of eye contact said only 'right, well,' and walked back inside. She laughed so much on telling the story that she snorted like a pig, and on noticing her snort she began laughing uncontrollably, snorting more. 'Right, well,' she kept repeating through her hysterical laughter. I couldn't help but catch the laughter bug and I laughed as much and as loudly as I can remember ever doing so. There were a few snorts from me too with each snort making the next one harder to suppress.

I tried to keep the conversation on Chantelle, about her life as much as possible. That was all I was interested in. I had no interest in telling her of my accountancy job, the fact that my dear old mum was struggling with her memory, or the suicide of my best friend. All those things would have killed the mood of a reunion that was to be celebrated. She spoke a lot about her children, not in the 'they're incredible and so smart' eye-rolling way that Hannah had and most people are prone to, but rather of the difficulties of parenting, the values she hoped to instil in her kids and the odd titbit about their personalities developing. And I actually, surprising myself somewhat, enjoyed hearing about them and what parenting was like for them. Her pregnancy that Thomas had announced when I last saw her, them, had produced a beautiful baby boy and, two years later, a sister for the young lad had been born. They were now seven and five years old respectively, and when she spoke of them, she couldn't help but smile. Her manner of speaking conveyed to me her love and pride in a refreshingly simple manner without any vacuous boasting of the kids' greatness. Indeed, she spoke of the little things that they did, like how little Sara, quite noisy most of the time I was informed, would sit in absolute silence, gazing curiously, whenever anybody would eat anything, or how Jonny would celebrate as though he'd scored a goal whenever his parents would announce that it was nice enough for him to go and play outside, causing his mum to regularly laugh hysterically in response. Often, I think people say how great their kids are because they want to show it's a reflection of how great they are. That can be overbearing and Chantelle's words about her children were clearly not to show off but rather a genuine reflection of her love for them. I really appreciated it, and it reminded me of all the small things that set her apart as somebody unique to me all those years ago.

While speaking of the kids and about life in general, it was notable to me that there wasn't any talk of Thomas. Eventually I asked Chantelle how he was; afterall, it was him that I was friends with originally, sort of, prior to her and I meeting. She paused, audibly and visibly inhaling and exhaling a deeper than usual breath on hearing my question. Her enthusiasm for conversation was lost in a moment.

'He's a wonderful father,' she repeated on multiple occasions over the next passage of conversation, and on witnessing her discomfort, I refrained from pressing her on Thomas or their relationship even though it was something I was curious about. Although I didn't glean much information about how they were doing as a couple, her lack of appetite to talk about him was a clear enough indication that my age-old suspicions, that they were not a pair made for one another, had been borne out.

To me it seemed, at first at least, as though Chantelle had lost her sense of wonder somewhat as though her passion for life, for causes, had been numbed by the passage of time. She was perhaps less chaotic in her thoughts, less rough around the edges, and seemingly less ready to pounce on any unthought-of out remark I would make. Having said that, I was trying incredibly hard not to say anything ill conceived, and for the most part, I succeeded. I felt no inclination to bait her into playful confrontation like I used to do from time to time. 'The problem with homeless people is they should have tried harder at school,' I might have said, grinning, to provoke a reaction. Indeed, I felt as though she probably had to listen to enough of that sort of thoughtless nonsense in the circles she now frequented, and so, with perhaps a rare display of wisdom on my part, I decided to keep things calm.

Initially, I found it difficult to decipher whether or not Chantelle's lack of fire was because she was more relaxed, because she was tired, or simply because she wasn't the same person I remembered. She wouldn't be that same person mind you, of course not, we all change, some for the better, and some for worse, in a kind of unavoidable self-evolution as, unable to halt the effects of our own experiences on our personalities, we become different from the person we've been. She was older, sure, not that much older, but her life had changed, she'd experienced what it is to care for children, and that had become her primary focus, maybe her sole focus. In those early exchanges, it seemed to me as though she'd perhaps admitted her lot in life that any of those social injustices that she used to speak about so breathlessly, so passionately, were of less interest to her.

Chantelle acknowledged that her children had and would continue to have every advantage in life, 'even more so than you!' she exclaimed in a jokey fashion as we became increasingly at ease with one another. She then followed it with reassuring words that reminded me of the old Chantelle as, in a determined fashion, with her face hardening that it was 'of the utmost importance that they would understand their position,' and that 'they will know that the family's wealth does not make them better or worse than anybody else.' Hearing those words gave me great satisfaction. Maybe it wasn't that she'd changed, but rather that she'd acknowledged her role had changed. Her focus had, quite naturally I guess, shifted, and I could imagine that she was an incredible mother, instilling in her children those principles which she would so vigorously discuss those years ago. She was now a teacher and I for one couldn't think of anybody better for any child.

It did briefly cross my mind as we sat down to have our cups of tea shortly after her arrival that Chantelle had come to see me in order to check whether there was anything between us, between us still. False hope dies hard. However, the way in which she spoke of her children made me instantly understand that she would never divorce Thomas, likely for the good of her kids, placing the stability of her family as more important than her own happiness. That was one of the only ways, possibly the only way, in which Chantelle could be regarded as a traditionalist. While I couldn't help but look at it so, I don't think Chantelle ever regarded staying with Thomas as a sacrifice but rather considered it as an extension of the decision she made when she got married in the first place.

Generally, I was successful in steering the conversation away from me with the exception being when Chantelle mentioned that one of the reasons she'd finally decided to come and visit was that Harry had told her of Sam's death. The two of them had met just the once I believe, again a pub engagement, quite naturally, so although she didn't know him well she knew that he was my best friend and that was 'enough for her to come' and ' to make sure her old friend was getting on okay'. 'Old friend.' It pained me to hear of myself spoken of in those terms, lumped in with the rank and file, and, on hearing that, I swiftly steered the conversation on to a different topic, which, for all my verbal inadequacies, is something I'm actually rather adept at doing. She told me how sorry she was for my loss and I brushed it off as 'part of life,' adding that 'unfortunately, death was a part of life that we all have to deal with, an aspect that is certain, definite, amongst all of the uncertainty that swirls around us in day-to-day life.'

However blunt it was, in an attempt to move the conversation on, that was probably one of the most philosophical sentences I've ever said. Indeed, Chantelle's eyes widened when I said it, as if she'd been waiting decades to hear something like that from me. It was an admission that I'd been thinking about life and death, the type of thinking that it feels both natural to have and natural to fight against. I had absolutely no inclination to discuss the potential role that our relationship, mine and Chantelle's had had on me being absent enough in my friendship with Sam to miss his suffering. I didn't, and wouldn't, want to ever burden anybody else with that, especially her, and frankly, I didn't want to dwell on it while she was there with me.

Disappointingly, Chantelle was only able to stay the one night on the island and was heading back on The Queasy Boat as she had nicknamed it the next morning. It was quite a journey to make for just the single night and I was extremely grateful, thankful really, that she had made the trip. I think she must have decided in advance that one night was the safest option in case of an unbearably awkward meeting, which thankfully hadn't come to fruition and when she left my house for her hotel, we hugged with a long, warm, meaningful embrace that I didn't want to end. I shed a tear, borne of a mixture of relief and happiness I think, which I attempted to quickly wipe away before she could see, failing to catch all of it as some partial tear trickled down my cheek. She would have almost certainly noticed it as she looked at me for a last time. We both knew no more words were necessary while we waved at one another as she left the house and walked down the street, soon round the corner and out of view.

There was, quite naturally, an immediate melancholic feeling of deflation in the aftermath of Chantelle leaving that mercifully soon passed, giving way to a sense of light contentment. The underlying anxiety that I had felt through almost an entire decade had, in the course of one enjoyable, love-filled evening, and one of the deepest sleeps I've ever known, dissipated in its entirety. To know that Charlotte had felt no anger or dislike towards me produced a great deal of peace of mind and rid me of the inner turbulence built on a loathing for myself that I'd gotten so used to over time, something that had led me to entirely forget what it was to have anything close to a satisfactory level of self-esteem or confidence. And, while things didn't seem to be going that well in her marriage, it gave me pleasure to know that she had found happiness with her children. She was content in her life and now, maybe I could be too.

While I don't have first-hand experience of the matter, it seems to me as though one of the hardest challenges in life must be to keep both parties happy and fulfilled in a long-term relationship. I have, in rare moments of reflection, contemplated that companionship may indeed be nice for me. However, while I can't help but wonder what could have been with Chantelle or even Hannah for that matter, a brief consideration of the people I know, or knew, reminds me of the pain or unhappiness, or boredom that seems to be abundant. Even my own parents, who I would class as a success story, a fairly happy pair, have not done very much talking to each other for more than a decade as far as I can tell as if they've run out of things to talk about. And now, after all those contented years together, my dad is having to watch my dear old mum lose her memory as he himself meanders towards the inevitability of what is likely to be a fairly lonely death. Maybe my relationship would be, or would have been different? Perhaps that is what everyone thinks.

Then again, when I think of old Sam and consider the way in which the isolation in his life led him to feel how he did, even an unhappy relationship might have made his life more bearable. Sure, I know now, as I knew then, that that sort of thinking is too simplistic; that the reasons for him doing what he did was more to do with a societal isolation and while I can never truly understand what he was going through, I can't help but think that if somebody had been there for him, to go home to him, it's possible that things may have turned out differently. Who knows?

My view on the subject has always been prone to uncertainty and change, often depending on my mood, how much I've had to drink, or perhaps how compelling somebody else's story or life of coupled happiness could be or at least seem. But for me, at least at the time of writing, my thoughts have become more settled as a new person in my life has given me a belief, or renewed belief, that relationships can work; Aoife.

10

Life trundled along as normal after Chantelle's visit. I fell back into my reclusive routine, invariably starting the day with a well-trusted Marmite on white toast and a large cup of instant coffee with a splash of milk each morning. Such a man of habit. When Tony Pizzini moved to the island, he could always be seen eating Marmite, equally as habitually as me, regardless of the fact that he thoroughly hated it. He'd decided, oddly, that it fitted well into his new British persona, which may have made sense on some level if anybody noticed, and, even if they did, they were likely just left wondering why he was eating something he clearly disliked as he grimaced and muttered in Italian under his breath while slowly, and painfully, chewing through the yeasty goodness. Tony, like most of us I guess, was of the opinion that the eyes of others were upon him, judging him, when the truth is that most people are just concerned about themselves.

My dear old mum, not one for Marmite herself, had been getting worse and worse, and there had begun to be a hollowness to her gaze as if, when speaking to me, she'd be looking straight through me. Indeed, on the increasingly rare occasions that she would speak, she spoke of the past as if it was more real to her than her present, in which life had seemingly become too confusing to try to make sense of. It was obvious to me that she knew she wasn't okay, but she was sharp enough of mind to act on clues; to guess about things she failed to remember and to laugh about things that she'd forgotten like it was normal, like it was a part of regular ageing. Occasionally, I would get frustrated about her laughing things off. I thought, wrongly no doubt, that Mum was ignoring her problem and so I'd put her under some pressure by asking questions so as to remind her that what was happening was problematic. To try and laugh her way out of the uncomfortable reality that she was losing her memory was, I know now, a form of coping mechanism, but at the time I found her lack of willingness to admit she had a problem to be quite infuriating. I think now that my dislike of her way of dealing was more a reflection of my inability to accept seeing her like that.

One of the many times that Mum'd forgotten where she'd put her glasses I decided to try and get her to retrace her steps, asking her what she'd done during the morning. Of course, she didn't know but I kept pursuing it, trying to get her to remember and to admit that she didn't know as she laughed, 'these things will happen to you when you get older,' she said with a careless and now frequent giggle. My pursuit of an acknowledgement by her that something was wrong didn't work and instead of accepting what was happening she turned to an agitated state, getting flustered and angry. Indeed, not long ago when asking her some questions she even swore at me when I tested her on what we'd eaten for dinner. 'Little shit,' she said in a tone I'd never encountered before and a glazed look in her eyes that didn't make her look like my mum. She'd always been so mild mannered and to see her lose her temper in such an uncharacteristic way was deeply upsetting, perhaps even more so for my dad.

My poor old dad was, understandably, struggling with the change in my mum, as I was too. He'd become prone to standing out the front of his house chain smoking menthol cigarettes hours on end, looking at nothing in particular, rain or shine. When I would see him out there, I would wonder what was going through his mind. I wondered if he was thinking about me, what he made of my life, whether he was happy with me. He, along with my dear old mum, gave me the opportunity to do so much, so much that he himself had not had the opportunity to do. I wondered if it crossed his mind that I'd wasted it. I wondered if he'd asked himself the question as to why I spent so little time with them. I've spent approximately half of my life living away from my parents and it has struck me recently as though that may have been time wasted, at least partially. By staying away from the island, I think I felt as though I was being slightly adventurous, that I'd be able to find something there, out in the world that I otherwise wouldn't - excitement, fulfilment, happiness dare I say. Indeed, I'd like to think that from time to time, I've been able to find those things, however fleeting, but whether it's been worth it, leaving my roots, my family, in search of nothing in particular, I'm uncertain.

In comparison to the sudden death of Sam, I was better mentally prepared in a way for what was happening to my dear old mum. At the back of my mind, I have, as we all do I suspect, contemplated the inevitability of what will happen to my parents as time, unable to be halted, whittles away. Indeed, when thinking about my mum, an old, somewhat bizarre conversation about the subject came to mind from when I was a child, on my birthday no less, possibly my seventh. It was a conversation between my dad, my highly rational, thoughtful dad, and my strange, often reckless, Uncle Peter. I was told that Uncle Peter was not the reliable sort. 'So unreliable,' was the most common phrase I recall being used by family in conversation about Peter. It was probably quite unfair and overly judgemental. My own memories are fond ones.

Peter was, characteristically it seemed, quite drunk on this occasion, and was asking my dad, in a taunting fashion, about whether he would 'get me' if my parents died. On the face of it, it doesn't sound that funny now but at the time, with the way he spoke to my dad, winding him up, winking at me as he did, smiling with his horrible grey teeth, it was really quite amusing. My dad didn't entertain the possibility at the start but then, after a while, he broke under continual questioning and indicated it would be auntie so and so to take care of me. Peter would act appalled, as if it was unexpected, asking me if that's what I wanted, winking at me again and I'd play along, giggling loudly and say, in no uncertain terms, that it wasn't. He'd carry on and then say, 'well I never, so after her, if she croaks, it'd have to be me next right?' I remember my dad would roll his eyes and vehemently say no, and then after more prodding from Uncle Peter would have to come up with another name. Again, he'd say aunt so and so, maybe great aunt so and so, whom I'd never heard of. The game would repeat and Peter would act appalled again and, to my dad's annoyance, the whole process would begin again. After about seven people, my dad finally gave in and said if all those people died that he could look after me, at which point he lifted me up and celebrated gleefully, running around our small garden with me over his head as I laughed uncontrollably. What a great guy. He was fun, and he, perhaps unwittingly, got me starting to appreciate the inevitability of death. He died young.

The truth be told, I've always thought that out of my parents it would be my dad that would be first to pass. He's worked hard all of his life, often spending long hours doing manual work in his shop, and, what with the cigarettes as well, I didn't think he'd make it anywhere close to a grand old age. It's been a bit of a shock therefore to see my mum, seemingly so healthy, looking likely to be the first to go. My initial reaction, when she was so clearly deteriorating, was towards feeling sorry for myself but I've managed to pull myself out of my mental slump quite quickly, possibly for the first time, and put all my energies into helping my dad through what has been a more difficult time for him. I know that I probably can't begin to understand what he is, has been, going through, having to watch the love of his life wasting away at glacial speed but loss is something I've known in my life, and although I think every loss is different, I believe I've been able to appreciate the sort of pain that he has been going through, been able to empathise with his situation and I'm confident that my presence alone can act as a source of comfort for him. I have been round to my parents as much as I could and helped out with things around the house. I've even helped out in the shop so that my dear old dad could either spend time with Mum or just have some much needed time to himself. We never have spoken too much to one another and even through this period, things have been no different. There was a comfort in our silences though, one that comes with the shared knowledge that talking isn't a necessity. They were much like the periods of silence that I used to have with Sam, and, like then, my dad and I have been content simply by being in one another's presence.

11

Life seemed to stagnate for me following Chantelle's visit with my activities limited to helping out my parents, and it must have been a full and uneventful two years before something noteworthy happened.

I'd gotten back home from working with my dear old dad out in the store one pleasant midsummer's evening, quite late, just as the sun was setting, to find a young girl waiting on my front lawn. She was quite striking, taller than I was, unsurprisingly, with long silky dark ginger hair, pale skin, and reflective light blue eyes. I parked the car and, as I got out, asked if I could help her.

'Good evening,' she said in a respectful tone but nervous manner, unable or unwilling to look me in the eye.

'It is. A lovely evening,' I responded cheerfully.

'My name is Aoife and I think that you are my dad.'

She said it abruptly, with the initial nervousness in her voice replaced with a rehearsed steel. I was taken aback. My legs turned to jelly and my breathing became heavy and awkward. I couldn't respond and drew on all the little strength I had to get myself inside in order to sit down. It was, after Chantelle's surprising arrival, the second time I'd truly felt old, as if I was entirely unable to deal with any slight shock, like any slight surprise could entirely derail the sensitive ecosystem my body had become. I just about managed to get some words out.

'Come in,' I said in a quick, panicked manner as, mustering all my barely adequate strength and concentration I opened the front door and entered the sanctuary of my home. After entering, I opened the first door on the right and sat down in the lounge. I sat to better pull myself together.

'I'm sorry, I'm very sorry,' I said, 'this is wholly unexpected.' As characteristically inadequate as the words were, they were true. I was genuinely sorry at that moment and all I could think was that my reaction, one of stress, must have been disappointing to her, that she must have been immediately disappointed by me. Apologising probably made me seem even more pathetic. Beyond that, I didn't know what to say and there was an awkward silence as I attempted to regain my breath and a sense of calm. I was, quite naturally, unable to think of what to say and mercifully, Aoife took the lead.

Aoife could see, very clearly no doubt, that I was struggling with the enormity of the situation. She tried to put me at ease and I'll forever be thankful for that effort. On seeing my own anxiety her nervous demeanour appeared to dissipate as she told me calmly 'not to worry.' Further proof that everybody else is better than me, more controlled, and far superior with finding the right words in these important scenarios. I remember the way she smiled at me, perhaps instinctively knowing that it would be a method to calm me down.

'Don't worry,' she said again, simple but effective, 'there's really no need to be flustered - I just wanted to visit you. I've been curious to meet you, but I don't want anything from you,' she said, with a double negative. I think she thought I wanted to hear that last part and I wish it hadn't had such a calming effect on me, to know that she didn't want anything from me, but it did. Her soft Irish accent was further comforting.

Who, how and what questions swirled around my head but they were tempered by the way Aoife conducted herself and I could tell intuitively that she was the switched on sort, aware of everything and everyone around her. Her obvious smarts, her instinct to notice and understand how I was feeling, and her ability to respond accordingly, reminded me of Sam.

'Oh, okay, right, thank you,' I responded meagrely. It pains me to write it now and I get distinctly embarrassed whenever I think back to it, which I try not to do. I offered her a cup of tea, which gave me time, more time, to go and attempt to compose myself in the kitchen. A refuge. Aofie took it with milk and sugar, just like me, which I found oddly comforting at the time. I remember telling myself that this was just as big a deal for her as it was for me, if not bigger, probably bigger, and that I should try and at least fake composure in order to help her through it. It has always seemed terribly natural to only think of myself even though I'm well aware that it might be, probably would be, beneficial to everybody, myself included, to not do so.

'So Aoife,' I said, smiling and upbeat in a forced attempt to act relaxed, 'that's a lovely Irish accent you have. Does that mean that Siobhan is your mother?' I think I may have pulled off a rare moment of nonchalance. Her face lit up and she chuckled.

'Yeah, that's right. I had a bet with her that you'd be able to guess whose daughter I was. She disagreed; she said you were too much of a lothario to remember.' She grinned at me, saying it in amusement rather than judgement.

'I definitely wouldn't say that,' I cringed as I recognised the truth in my response, 'I've always been fairly clueless with women, I mean look at me now.' I wasn't sure whether I was referring to right now, in that moment, or now more generally. Regardless, I gained confidence with every passing moment of conversation. 'Of course I remember your mum.' The truth is that even a small number of people are difficult to remember twenty or so years later, especially when a different woman dominated your thoughts for so long. Siobhan was, however, a girl I certainly remember; witty, smart, not to mention beautiful, and, quite naturally therefore, way too good for me. We'd had a great couple of weeks together, but that was all unfortunately. When we'd met, she was heading back to Ireland at the end of doing a Masters Degree in Political Science, and our short and sharp romance, if you could call it that hadn't seemed to warrant either of us turning our lives upside down. Clearly though, our brief liaison had had a more long-standing impact on one of our lives.

Once what was going on had finally started to settle in, for it does tend to take me a long while to process things, I was quite astounded that Siobhan hadn't contacted me, slightly offended even. It's true that I don't know what I'd've done in her situation but I'm pretty sure I would've done something to let the other person know. The first thought that came to my mind was that maybe she didn't think I was worth it; perhaps that it'd be better, easier, without me. It seemed natural for me to go instantly to the most depressing answer. I could have loved her, loved them for certain, and I said as such to Aoife, well, I replaced the loving part with help. I could have helped. Maybe. I rather sheepishly, with it now my turn to be unable to hold eye contact, asked her why her mum had never got in contact with me. Apparently, she'd lost my phone number. It wasn't the first time I'd heard that one but I was not inclined to distrust Aoife or Siobhan for that matter. I recall having written my phone number down for Siobhan when we had met for the first time but she'd misplaced it sometime through the next couple of weeks. On being unable to contact me readily, she'd taken the decision that it wasn't a good idea to return to London to drop such a bombshell on me and on my life. I was thankful I guess, but I'll forever wonder about the different trajectory my life could have taken had she let me know.

Aoife was clearly pleased that I'd remembered her mum and, with my hands no longer shaking and the blood that had been pumping rapidly around my head receding, we both became visibly more relaxed. My face even returned to normal having spent at least forty-five minutes a deep shade of pink. Aofie had found me through finding and messaging people who had gone to my university around the same time, friends of mine, one of the details that her mother had remembered about me. After blanket messaging hundreds of people, she got a positive response from a man named Harry Brown. What? Harry again, what a guy, I couldn't believe it. He has managed to play an outsized role in my life, considering he's a man I don't really know all that well. Indeed, when I heard that it was him that informed Aoife, I didn't know whether to get in touch with him and thank him or to call the police and report him as a stalker. Odd bloke but a good friend.

According to Aoife, Siobhan wasn't too keen on the idea of her finding me, fearing the worst about how I would react, and she didn't want to come herself. Aoife's curiosity however, so she told me, was unstoppable, and she couldn't help but want to come and see me. 'To check me out.' As she said with another disarming grin.

'You remind me of somebody,' I said, as we moved outside and had our second cup of tea.

'Oh yeah. My mum perhaps?' she enquired in a teasing fashion.

'Well, yes, but no, that's not who I was thinking of,' I said. 'It's actually an old friend of mine, a really very good friend actually. He was as sharp as a tack and had a clear instinct for putting people at ease.' Sharp as a tack was a strange turn of phrase and, as soon as I'd said it, I knew that it would make me seem my age, and older perhaps.

'That's grand, high praise,' she said, blushing, 'perhaps I can meet him and we'll both feel at ease easily,' she jested once more, with what seemed to be very natural wit.

'If only I wish that were possible. He passed away a few years ago regrettably.' Even though plenty of time had passed, saying those words aloud, acknowledging his passing is something I'd rarely done, still have rarely done, and it filled me with agony. Aoife noticed my anguish and pain, of course she did, and she got up to put her hand on my shoulder. The truth be told, I'd gotten so used to comforting my dear old dad in the recent years that I'd forgotten what it was to be comforted myself. It was such a simple act but it was as though it released something in me. My face scrunched up, reddening, and a tear trickled down my cheek. 'Thank you,' I whispered.

Aoife had been due to stay at a hotel in the town centre but I had the spare room and so was having none of it. She was only staying one night on the island and I wanted to spend every available moment I could with her. Indeed, as the fear subsided it left behind the rarest of things in my life, a genuine, let's not go to sleep, let's stay awake as long as we can child-like excitement. Plus, it was no problem for me to put her up in a room that was barely used. She duly obliged me by staying and I was thrilled, cracking a smile and putting the kettle on again. The briefness of her stay reminded me of when Chantelle came, and I couldn't help but notice the similarity. I wished they'd both stayed for longer.

While from time to time there has been the very occasional visitor to the house, I'd become used to being alone for long periods and had all but forgotten what it was like to just share space and time with somebody else, whether that be in conversation, laughter or silence. I didn't know Aoife, it is true, but I felt at home with her, almost as though this wasn't the first time she'd been to the house, or indeed the first time we'd met.

'You seem a very thoughtful person,' I remember her saying, to break a short silence.

'Perhaps,' I said with an involuntary sigh.

'Well, I think that is an admirable trait. Most people just open their mouths and don't really mind what comes out.' I couldn't have agreed more with her, but I myself was too far the other way; whatever the opposite is of a chatterbox or a vacuous gossip and I said as such.

'That's true, but you don't want to think too much about things, if you think too much you become poor at speaking.' She laughed thinking I was joking.

'No, it's true,' I said. 'If you think too much, it's often because you want what you say to be perfect, but what any of us says is rarely perfect, and that either means you don't say anything at all or you end up stumbling over your words trying to say something perfectly.' I sighed again. 'At least that's what it's like for me anyway, maybe I can't think fast enough.' I semi-joked that time.

'You've probably got a point,' Aoife said.

'Well, thinking is something I think I think I can actually talk about without thinking,' I quipped, maybe poorly. She looked at me with a raised eyebrow and I laughed, she followed suit. 'Yes,' I said, 'that was an attempt at humour.'

I've never thought of myself as having any wisdom at all really, and the idea that somebody would want to listen to me talk about my life and the things, the lessons that I'd learnt was wholly alien to me. But, I have to say, I got a real thrill out of it. Indeed, I'd never really considered myself to have lived a particularly interesting life but it turns out that just by making it to a certain age, things that seemed mundane, like love, death and personal failings can be interesting to somebody young. We talked about Sam a bit, well, I spoke, combining my memories of our friendship with words about the importance of being healthy in your own head. I even started talking about the importance of owning your own thoughts and being comfortable with them. I think it was mostly nonsense I was saying and I wish Sam had been there to explain it better. I like to picture him looking down on me chuckling as I struggled to remember the things he used to discuss in those often one-way discussions with me.

Aoife engaged with me and had her own tales to tell of her experiences and those of her friends, on the mental pressures that life can have, of exam stress, fitting in at school and parental expectations. It is true that the younger generations are more open to talking about these things, but it seems to me as though, even with being more comfortable to share their feelings, people have somehow become more isolated from one another. There are so many individuals and so few units, so few close families, so few communities. It seems like a natural slide, an unavoidable evolution into individualism and isolation, and yet it appears as though it's a conscious choice we are all making, unable to resist, regardless of the known pitfalls.

Aoife and I discussed relationships and love of all things, which was something I'd never done before, certainly not sober anyway. She spoke of a boyfriend and I remained fairly quiet not wanting to put her off by speaking in too cynical a manner. My experience of relationships was my experience and who is to say that hers wouldn't be different. Silence, so natural to me, was a wise option. She seemed to pity me, not in her words, but in her body language as she looked around the house that was clearly in need of a loving touch, hopelessly lacking in family photos, missing any tasteful design, and with two house plants in the lounge that were on the way to the big compost heap in the sky. I didn't enjoy it at all, but maybe I should be pitied. Indeed, from time to time I do pity myself for ending up alone without anybody to share my life with, without companionship.

The next morning, before Aoife's flight, we went for a walk on the beach on the island's west coast, about a ten-minute stroll away from my house. It was windy and the water unseasonably cold but the sky was bright blue and it was too tempting not to at least put our feet in the water. We took off our shoes and rolled up our trousers, wading in to about shin height. My feet went numb in seconds and I quickly got out again while Aoife stayed an extra minute or so. 'Ah, it's nothing compared to the west coast of Ireland,' she said cheekily. Maybe I'm getting soft as I get older. It was on the slow meander back to the house that Aoife suggested I write a book.

'Nobody would be interested in anything I have to say,' I said in a response that felt natural to me, avoiding eye contact, looking to the floor. As I said it though a great deal of shame washed over me. I'd been so aloof for so long and content with not really doing much that when I said aloud that nobody would be interested in my life it was really quite sad. I'm not sure whether Aofie noticed my distress after I said it. She probably did.

'Well just write it for me then,' she responded. 'You said you're not the most eloquent, but maybe writing your thoughts down, your experiences, would be good, even just as an exercise.'

'But what would I write about?' I asked.

'I don't know,' she said. 'I was hooked on your every word when we were talking last night, write that down, talk about Sam, of mental health, his and yours and talk about your fears and regrets.'

After instant reticence to the idea, I rather inexplicably promised that I'd write that book and a week after she left back for Ireland, I started it. This is it, and there is indeed something special about the process, making me feel as though whatever it might have been, whatever hardships that I have been through, they may have actually been worthwhile as now, finally perhaps, I've been able to learn from them during this process of reflection, gaining a certain degree of self-awareness. Indeed, certain realisations have occurred to me while I've been considering the past, and I hope that any small amount of wisdom I've gained has been adequately put on paper. I've tried to be honest, about myself, what's affected me, who's affected me, and how it's caused me to be, to change, to evolve.

Writing about the past has even made me think of the future, something I hadn't done for a long while. Somewhere, after the death of Sam, maybe before in fact, I'd settled for comfort over anything else and now, for the first time, I've realised that I have regrets. People often say that they regret the path not travelled, the road not taken, or something like that. For me, I'm starting to regret not following any real path at all, continually opting for the bench on the path that I was already sat on. It's been a comfortable bench for certain, but I should have wandered away from it at least a little.

Part Three - Pretty Old

12

After an initial flurry of writing, largely unreadable, frenzied writing really, plenty of time has passed, often involving me staring blankly at a piece of paper, trying to remember any interesting activity or thought worthy of writing down in the recent past. Unfortunately, it turns out that smiling to myself geekily as I hazily recall something from earlier in the week or month is not the same as committing words to a page in a coherent, or at least partially coherent manner.

As Mum's condition has grown increasingly dire, helping her and helping out my dad, keeping him company, has dominated my time. Around three months after Aoife's glorious visit, during that period of the early winter when the sun hangs low and the days shorten all too quickly, my poor old mum's memory was diminishing as fast as the daylight hours. She began not just to forget things that had happened recently but was also, from time to time, failing to recognise people. Initially, it was the regular postman, a short and stocky man with an earring and a good mane of hair on him who she'd've spoken to with regularity over the last couple of years. He was a jovial sort of guy who, not taking his job too seriously would often stop to have a chat with anybody sitting in the small garden at the front of the house.

'Hello Mrs. D, old little D,' he joked, referring to my mum and I as he stepped through the front gate on a bright but torturously cold late morning. I laughed as I felt obliged to do, and then caught sight of my mum with a face awash with vacancy. She clearly knew she was meant to know him.

'Oh hello…' she responded, unable to find the name.

'Darren,' he interjected, laughing hesitantly, 'only been your postie for two years now, have a lovely day everyone.' He shimmied off to the next house and I could see the concern in my mum's face, frowning with consternation at what had happened.

Mum's recognition of who people were and what their relationship to her was deteriorated quickly from that day and, all too soon after the postman incident, she failed to recognise who I was. It's something that I knew would likely come, but a part of me thought I'd be special. She'd always recognise me surely, I was her little boy after all. I'd come round to help my dad out in the garden as I did often and had twice already that week. I gave a 'good afternoon Mum' to her as she sat in the lounge and gave her a kiss on the cheek. I noticed something, that vacancy again, and with it, my heart dropped from my chest plummeting to my stomach. I felt the need to say that it was me as Darren the postie had done.

'It's me, you know me Mum,' I said it as a half statement, half question, hoping to prompt some acknowledgement.

'Oh yes, hello darling,' she said after a few seconds of delay, still with the vacancy on her face, appearing to stare through me. That was it, no point of return; it continued to happen on every occasion after that day too. She would sometimes say nothing and at others, she would say that I couldn't be me, that 'her dear Walter' was much younger, more athletic. I'd roll my eyes trying not to take it too badly. 'My dear Walter has hair,' she said once. Often, there was something in the way she would look at me that hinted at recognition, the type of curious gaze that you or I might give someone that we recognised but couldn't quite place.

A great deal of time passed at the beginning with the memory loss and illness taking hold of mum seemingly happening in a slow manner, but from forgetting who the postman was to not being able to remember too much at all, time passed quickly. Indeed, her failure to remember how to do things grew so bad that she needed help dressing, cleaning her teeth and going to the toilet only a matter of weeks after the first time she failed to recognise me. When I would help her, particularly in the period prior to things getting so bad that she was incapable of doing the simplest of daily tasks, she would get agitated and angry and tell me to leave. My instinct is that the agitation displayed an understanding within her of what was happening, even if she was unable to communicate that acknowledgement. I knew that it was a demonstration of her frustration at what was happening, a clue as to how she was feeling underneath the confusion, as it was when I used to test her memory. It was soul destroying to watch, and as much as I knew that those moments, those clashes, were a result of her fear and frustration they still hurt me deeply. Those I knew were our last moments together and there she was, all her fear and pain manifesting itself as anger towards me.

The anger and the frustration my mum showed towards me hurt, but it was nothing compared to the pain felt when I saw my dear old dad after she'd failed to recognise him one late afternoon. The trauma of that moment was such that it'll likely forever be a memory etched into my mind. Even the smallest of details will likely remain vivid to me, the dark green knitted jumper he wore and the shade of purple the bags under his eyes were.

It was a bitterly cold February day, dry but freezing, literally, and Dad and I had been outside in the garden for an hour or so doing some weeding and watering, trying to keep it presentable. It was in the afternoon and the sun was about to disappear when it happened. Even though I was wearing gloves, my hands were numb from the cold and I'd been putting them under some warm water to try and get some dexterity back. I'd lost all feeling in my fingers and it took a few seconds to tell whether the water was warm or cold. While I had my right hand under the tap, I heard my father say, 'Oh fuck no. No, no, no, no, no.' I'd never heard my dad swear before and, as such, I knew in an instant that something was deeply wrong. He always wanted to set a good example for me and that didn't change regardless of whether I was five or fifty years old.

My dear old mum had recognised my dad about six weeks longer than me, even after losing the ability to do many things, and when it happened, when she recognised him no more, I saw something for the first and only time in my life. He left the room and entered the kitchen, flicked the kettle on, sat down and tears streamed and streamed and streamed down his face. He was silent, entirely silent, he didn't look at me or anything, he looked straight ahead, as if looking at nothing. He made no attempt to wipe his face dry, the tears seemingly endless, as if drawn from an infinite reservoir of pain. Even when I went to comfort him, when I stooped down to hug him while he was in the chair, he didn't say anything. He continued on, looking straight ahead. For him I believe, his life, the point of his life, finished then. His will to do anything more ceased. He was old and frail and looking after my mum had taken a tremendous physical toll on him. But that, that moment, was when mentally he gave up.

13

Yesterday was Mum's funeral. After that solemn evening when she failed to recognise my dad we decided, with heavy hearts, that maybe it was for the best if we put her into a nursing home in order that she could get better help than that we were able to provide her. Partly it felt selfish, like we'd been taking on too much and we'd given up, given up on her to make life easier on us. But I think it was the only option. We were beaten. My mum didn't recognise us and my dear old dad was broken. The last few years had aged him twenty and any lease of life that he'd had, any drive to keep living, to learn, to provide, to explore, had been taken from him. Mum had soldiered on for a couple of months in the home before a torturous, seemingly never-ending, three-week stay in the hospital with her body shutting down on her. For me and my dad, the grieving had begun well before her death, perhaps even before she'd begun to fail to recognise those around her and the character of pain that I felt was different to that following the shock loss of Sam, where the depth of feeling was driven by the instant nature of the event with no time to prepare for the finality of death.

When Mum finally passed there was great sadness, but it was tinged with relief that the ordeal was over, both for her and for my dear old dad. For me these feelings of sadness, of loss, have been accompanied with a regret, a strong regret that comes with the knowledge that so much time that could have been spent with her had been wasted.

The truth is that for many years the relationship between my mum and I, my parents and I really had been a loving one but of distanced love. It was my fault entirely. They were my decisions, and while I could always count on them, the strength of our relationship and the power of our love was tempered by geography. Then even when I moved back to the island, in the immediacy of Sam's death, I would only visit once a month, if that. That was for no reason in particular other than laziness, I had nothing better to do, and yet time always drifted, as is its tendency. I should have spent more time with her and I'll never know whether she was unhappy with me for moving away, for not being there for so many years. Maybe it contributed to her anger? I don't know. I should've spent more time with her. She would allude to it when I lived in London, to her want for me to come home without ever explicitly telling me to do so. It would always be framed as though it would be for me, as opposed to anything to do with her. 'Wouldn't you be happier back here?' or 'wouldn't it be nice for you to come home and relax?' she used to ask politely, without pressure, even though I knew that she wanted me to come home, understandably I guess, for her own sake. I think now that I was selfish to stay away and now it's lost on me as to why I did.

It would have actually been quite nice for me to spend a couple of years, during my thirties perhaps, living on the island, when my parents were younger. Why I was quite so reticent to do so seems trivial now; I was afraid of the boredom there might have been when I should have embraced the tranquillity that I now cherish.

Not just yesterday, at the funeral, but in the months previous too I have seen my dad's anguish from a suffocatingly close proximity. It has been so visceral, easily witnessed in his every movement that I've been wondering how that level of pain, borne out of spending a lifetime together, could ever be worth it. The closest comparison I could ever think of is whether my relationship with Sam was worth the pain that consumed me when he died. It seems, quite simply I guess, the greater the level of friendship, or the deeper the level of love, the greater the level of heartache, of pain. For so long, ever since I fell for Chantelle, I've been uncertain as to whether that suffering is worth the love that precedes it. But I know now that I'd never have taken back my friendship with Sam for anything, and I dare say that my dear dad would do it all again.

Indeed, it's been many years now I've spent, quite naturally it seemed, protecting myself from the possibility of any more pain, the pain of losing somebody else I cared for or the pain of being rejected by somebody. But as I sit in my lonely house, devoid of the presence of somebody else, singing in the shower, rustling in the kitchen, or playing some music, I would swap any amount of rejection or loss for companionship, for friendship, for love.

Death is a strange one. That's not very profound. The inevitability of death is something that I've been generally familiar with, perhaps thanks to my Uncle Peter's morbid jokes, yet I've generally spent most of my time ignoring its possibility, at least in the near future, like many people I guess. Indeed, it's as true for me as anybody else that I thought I was invincible when I was younger and, although I was aware of the chance of those older than me and close to me dying, it's not something that occupied my mind a great deal. My first experience of death was when my grandfather died, and that sadness and mourning for the passing of a man I adored gave me a level of preparation for future loss.

Now, with a shaky hand and a churning in my stomach, it's sadly come time to write of the passing of my dear old dad. He did so just under a year after my mum had done so, without any fanfare whatsoever, just as he would have liked it. He'd grown pretty weak physically, but mercifully his mind was still in good shape, and he was able to live in his cottage that my parents had bought about thirty years ago all the way until his final hour. I got a slightly concerned call from a neighbour, whose name escapes me, saying that he'd gone round for a cup of tea as he did every couple of days or so, and hadn't received a response at the door. I went round, opened up with my spare key, and there he was, in bed, the colour of life drained from him. I called an ambulance, not that anything could be done, and later I was told that he'd passed away peacefully during the night. He'd had a good innings and I felt relatively content with his passing. I have no idea what happens after death and would never be bold enough to claim that I do, but it's given me some comfort to know that he no longer had to mourn my mother's passing. Instead, perhaps, he could be with her somewhere, in peace.

My dad had always been physically strong and I think now that perhaps, to keep you going, you need a mental will as well. It's almost as if it's some sort of desire of the brain to continue with life that can keep the other organs going. I dare say there is no science whatsoever to back up this claim, but, in my experience, it seems to be the way. Sure, my dear old dad did grow, or shrink, to be physically weaker as he looked after my mother in her final years, but still he looked to be reasonably strong and he was still more than able when it came to working in the garden doing jobs that involved some strength. I remember being in the garden with him just a few months prior to my mum's passing and commenting on how impressed I'd been with him ripping a sizable, deeply rooted weed out of the turf with his bare hands. I think it is entirely fair to say therefore, that his lack of will to live contributed to the swiftness of his death after my mum's. I don't say this with any degree of ill feeling. Of course not. He loved me dearly, but she was his companion for life, she was the one he spent almost every day with for fifty years or so, and, without her being around, the void in his life was so great that it's understandable and forgivable that he didn't know how to go on, or summon the energy to continue.

My parents had me young and I think them being young and able had perhaps been a reason in me feeling few qualms with moving away from the island and staying away. I owe them a lot for the early life they provided me and the manner in which they let me pursue what I wanted, even if I wasn't entirely sure what that was. If you were to think of things in terms of society and class, like Chantelle used to do, endlessly, they were definitely enablers of the family moving up the ladder, if it is a ladder. I was the first in our family to go to university and one of the first, if not *the* first, I'm not sure, to have a life which didn't involve working with the hands, blue collar work. I guess it's not all their own doing. It's true that things changed around them, in the economy on the island, which meant their hard work paid well enough to create comfort, perhaps unlike generations before.

Even so, I like to think it was their efforts in particular, their hard work, that have made my life a comfortable one, at least in terms of money. And, I'm thankful for that, although it's tinged with a guilt that comes with knowing that I probably haven't made the most of it.

I'd never looked a lot like either of my parents; at least I didn't think I did. Often Sam would say that I got my big nose from my dad, but I'd always thought my dear old dad's nose was twice as big. Now when I look in the mirror I can see the resemblance. I haven't been eating much or sleeping as much as I should and my frame has shrunk a lot. That, combined with the lack of forestation on my head, means the eye has a tendency to be drawn to the nose, which, as the mirror will attest to, looks bigger than ever.

Even through the fairly short period since Charlotte's visit, six, seven years or so, I've transformed again, going back the other way, losing my weight. I'm not slim and toned as I used to be though, more slim and frail, and while my hair seems to have no problems continuing to grow on the side of my head, the top of my head is increasingly barren, well entirely barren. I've become, in what is increasingly old age, the spitting image of my father. There could be worse people to imitate I guess, and if I can age as gracefully and nobly as he did, I think, in that, I'll take a degree of self-satisfaction with me to the grave. While my dad's grief for my mother was heart-breaking, a small silver lining, if there could ever be one, is that it's given me a renewed belief in the idea that love between two people can be sustained through a lifetime. I had been of the opinion that love was obsessed over and then lost once found and then replaced with strange things like pets and babies in a desperate bid to recapture what was gone. Most relationships, once loving perhaps, seem clearly to have a shelf life, assuming the notion of what they regard as being love itself isn't just an imagined poor equivalent in the first place. Their own version. How do you ever know? As big Tony Pizzini used to say, 'feelings are relevant.' While Tony, beyond his years in many ways, was probably, well definitely true to say feelings are relevant, in this context he meant relative, relative to you. Indeed, I can't say for certain that what I used to feel, the 'love' for Chantelle was akin to what my dear old mum and dad felt for one another. Perhaps they'd had something stronger, indeed maybe there *are* grades of love and what I felt for Chantelle I confused for something greater; confused my feelings for what I'd seen advertised, written about, spoken about. That said, when we met up again after years apart, my aged heart, struggling away, thudded harder than it had ever done. Maybe that was proof of love. I've never found anything since, anyone since, to make that happen, and now perhaps it's all too late. My failure to look for anything, to 'put myself out there' as they say, has become another source of regret.

To content myself with the realisation that it's too late to find love, or to find love again, is something that I'm coming to terms with. Aoife could be a source of love, at least in terms of family love, an altogether different sort, grade, but certainly more reliable with regards to its endurance. I received a message from her shortly after my dear old dad passed away saying that she and her mum were thinking about visiting and would be keen to visit during the next summer. Would I be happy to show them around the island? I responded immediately to that. Of course, it would be my pleasure to show them around and her and her mum could stay with me if they so wished for as long as they fancied. A desperate response perhaps but my lonely heart beat a little faster when I read that message. I was excited. What a rarity. I would gladly take the settee while Siobhan could have my room and Aofie could have the spare bedroom. She insisted that they couldn't do that to me but I insisted back that it would be of no problem at all and she bent to my will. Sleeping on the settee won't be great but when I can't suck that sort of thing up for a couple of nights to make somebody else's life a bit more comfortable the end truly is closing in!

14

'How's the book coming along?' Aoife said with a raised and excited voice accompanied by a big smile after spotting me as she came through the arrivals hall at the airport. Walking towards me she cracked that mischievous grin that I'd become accustomed to during our first meeting. I laughed, it was an icebreaker and I appreciated it as my nerves subsided quickly. It was great to see her and, with the ice broken, we were able to seamlessly continue where we'd left off almost two years earlier, which was perfect. A lot of time had passed and a lot had happened in my life since then with the passing of both my parents.

'It's coming, sort of,' I responded in a non-committal way. I think she was surprised that I'd even started and on noticing her surprise, I sent a knowing and slightly smug 'weren't expecting that' look her way. The truth is that I have my sights set on finishing it soon, hopefully with a happy ending. Ideally, I want the ending of my story to be an 'into the sunset' kind of deal, a move away from the island. I think I'm ready. I'd like to settle somewhere warm and sunny with an abundance of rum-based cocktails and open-air bars. Maybe I could even learn another language, if I should be so bold.

After my dad's death I decided to retire from work, perhaps I should have done it sooner and while for the last few years I've been able to work part-time, meaning that the hours haven't caused me too much strain, I'm okay for money and need not carry on. Indeed, I've inherited my parent's cottage and am able to rent it out for a very reasonable sum. With little expenditure, I'm lucky enough to have more money than I require. It's a highly privileged position that I find myself in, one that I've known I'll have my whole life. The knowledge that my parent's own property would one day become mine has always given me a level of financial security when I've considered what my money situation would be like when I got old. It's a position that I'd wrongly assumed everybody had when I was younger and I'm now, only recently really, embarrassingly appreciative of my situation. I think that Chantelle would be proud that I've finally achieved some degree of self-awareness. Maybe I'll even do something with such privilege one day.

'Did your mum decide against the trip then?' I said, becoming a little anxious again.

'No, she's just waiting for her bag, she's coming,' Aoife responded, smiling widely with her thick, curiously dark, eyebrows raised. Awaiting Siobhan wasn't quite the same feeling as when I found Chantelle at my front door but, nevertheless, I had a nervous anticipation and my heart was, as it has a propensity to do, pounding. Indeed, the thudding in my chest and the expenditure of nervous energy caused a shortness of breath and I had to sit. I would do more exercise but I'm afraid that at this stage it could well do more damage than good.

My memory of how she used to look wasn't entirely clear, grainy at best, perhaps understandably, and when Siobhan came through the arrivals door, I didn't really recognise her. Her once golden hair was now a distinguished looking, thick light grey, which she wore up in a business-like style. She couldn't have looked more different than the hazy freeze-frame that I had in my mind, of her as an alternative, edgy student, adorned with a nose piercing, ripped jeans and regularly wearing the t-shirt of a band far from the mainstream. She was now wearing black boots, expensive looking, accompanied by tight black trousers with an elegant white, off-white blouse. It all came flooding back to me when I studied her face close-up while I, quite naturally, stumbled over what the right words to say were. I should really get something to say prepared for nerve-inducing occasions such as these. I think she must only be around six or seven years younger than me, but if a stranger would have been asked they would have easily put twenty years between us. She looked strong, fit, and powerful and as for me, well, I'm me.

'Hi,' Siobhan opened informally, Chantelle-esq, and in a quiet, timid manner that didn't really fit her look, 'so you've met our little creation?' she said, allowing herself a small smirk.

'I have, she's really quite something,' I said, perhaps in a manner that could have been mis-interpreted. She paused for a second then smiled a fuller smile and, while winking at her daughter, said,

'Yes, she is.' I think that Aoife must have let her know that I was likely to be nervous and unlikely to be able to find the perfect words. I'm grateful for her doing so. 'Shall we get going then?' she said.

'Absolutely,' I said affirmatively before I led them to the car park where my ageing chariot awaited. Unfortunately, we then spent a painstaking and almost entirely silent twenty minutes looking for my car as I attempted to recall where I'd parked it. Eventually I found it and took the two of them to my house to settle in. A great first impression.

It was a lovely, calm, sunny day so I thought it'd be nice for us to have a barbecue that evening. Both Siobhan and Aoife were, and are still no doubt, vegetarians. Aoife had only become one recently but Siobhan had become one back when she was in her twenties 'before it was fashionable' she joked, with a sense of pride. That scuppered my plan slightly but I was told that they could put vegetarian things on the barbecue and it would be just as good, 'maybe even better.' I was sceptical. I didn't hold being vegetarian against them even if, for a reason I'm not entirely sure of, it's a life choice that I naturally find annoying, maybe even intimidating. I had to go out and get some corn on the cob and they made a burger type patty thing from chickpeas, onion and some spices that had been in my cupboard for as long as I could remember. I tried a bite and while it certainly wasn't as good as the real thing, it didn't taste too bad at all. It's hard to admit to myself but I guess, maybe, the comparison between the way both of us looked could, almost certainly, be a testament to our differing lifestyles and eating habits. I'd happily blame it on genetics, so as to have a personally palatable excuse, but both of my parents were in fine shape and, surely enough, both would eat in a very responsible manner. I think it's too late for me to change now and to be honest, I'm not really sure I want to in almost any way. Indeed, I admire it, them, sure, but I am what I am and while self-improvement is nice to think about, it's a younger person's game. I lathered my burger, beef burger, in ketchup and cheese while washing it down with a couple of beers which was highly enjoyable and mercifully for all, it was accompanied by a regular level of flatulence instead of the raised level that can occasionally happen in response to the beers. A risk well taken.

Aoife and Siobhan stayed the weekend and, quite pathetically, it was probably the best two days of my life. They arrived on the Friday afternoon, leaving on the Sunday back to Dublin, and while my back was in pieces, figuratively, after spending a couple of nights on the settee, it didn't detract from what was a thoroughly enjoyable weekend. We were, bar a short shower on the Saturday afternoon, lucky with the weather and we were able to get about the island to a few nice spots, mainly to the white sand beaches on the west coast which create a glistening turquoise water when the sky is bright. As much as I love the island for all of its natural beauty it must be said that there's not much to do from an entertainment standpoint so good weather was crucial. Luckily, the wind was calm, the sun shone and it felt almost Caribbean, or how I imagine the Caribbean to feel. For the most part, I took a seat on my foldable chair while we were on the beach and was content enough just to watch on as the two of them would either head off into the sea for a swim or be hitting a tennis ball to one another on the harder sand. Aoife was very good with the tennis racquet in hand, a natural, and while watching her play it dawned on me for the first time that we had some genetic similarities. Indeed, her hand eye coordination was much better than her mum and she even ran a little bit like me with her left foot outwards, ruining the body's symmetry. The similarities to me were few though as, luckily for her, she'd inherited almost all of her features from her mother. Even in the freezing cold sea, Siobhan kept a certain elegance about her with her long limbs and her neat hair exuding a certain grace, traits and physical attributes which Aoife had inherited. Thankfully too, Aoife hadn't got my nose.

It was, has been, difficult to resist thinking, when watching them fooling around on the beach, of a life not lived, my alternative reality. What it may have been like if I'd done just one thing differently. I sat there, on the beach, with what must have looked like a gormless smile as my mind periodically slipped into daydream. We'd had something, however intangible and difficult to define, Siobhan and I, back when we'd met, but I'd never taken a chance, never rolled the dice, I'd been characteristically passive, waiting, always waiting for something to happen as opposed to making it happen. How easy would it have been to get over to Dublin just to see if there could've been anything more in our relationship?

It has always seemed quite natural to me to have an apathy towards doing, go-getting if you will, actively influencing the future and I wonder now, as I spend more time looking back than forward, why that desire for nothing, the acceptance of choosing the easy option, was my default setting. It's true that my general passivity has gotten greater as I've aged, but it's something, a trait I feel I've had from very young, at least on some level. I've always had a curious and unwavering belief that everything would just fall into place and that I wouldn't have to do anything, wouldn't have to make any effort to achieve whatever it was I wanted. It is perhaps, as I'm sure Chantelle would argue, the natural dial setting of a person born into a sheltered, secure, easy life. Still, I would see my parents working hard and I would assume that that wasn't something I needed to do - that wasn't for me. For my generation, things would be easier. Maybe they have been, but my comfort has informed my lack of aspiration and that has led me to live a life of very little, with only a few good memorable times, punctuated by a plethora of missed opportunity and regret.

It had been so many years since we'd last met that, as well as struggling to remember what she looked like, I couldn't really remember much about Siobhan's personality all together well. Indeed, as I get older I find that while I can recall my general opinion of a person as I judged them at the time, overly quickly no doubt, I struggle to remember the mannerisms they had or the things they did that built that opinion in the first place. I recall her being witty and sharp, switched-on you could say, but I can't remember why. There's no ingrained memory of a specific moment or day, or story I can recount that made me form that opinion. It must be that there are lots of small reasons for why a long-lasting feeling about a person is formed, things that don't necessarily register in the memory. And that decision as to what a person is, or was like and how they make or made us feel endures despite a lack of recollection as to why. I do think it's possible for people to change but the way people will do certain things, say things in a certain manner, the way they make you feel instinctively, that can't be altered much through time and Siobhan was a prime example. The languid way she moved, spoke without saying anything specific, and joked subtly with a pause and eye-contact to check if you'd understood her sharp wit hadn't changed over the years, and those idiosyncrasies triggered familiar feelings of fondness towards her, founded way back when.

Despite the instant familiarity, the weekend had started in a timid fashion, as if two strangers were meeting for the first time. It seemed a natural state of affairs, but gradually, as we got more comfortable with one another, we began to open up and talk more about our lives. I loved listening to Siobhan. She was ambitious in her professional life, becoming a special advisor on economic policy to the Irish government. I couldn't help but smile to myself when she was talking about herself, something she was endearingly reluctant to do, but something I encouraged. It was as if she was a blend of old economics guru Sam and the political Chantelle. It was an impressive job, an impressive career and I was really happy for her. I recalled it was the type of work that she'd wanted to do as a student and to witness somebody achieving what they'd set out to do in life seems to me to be something rare and worth celebrating. She didn't say as much, probably not wanting to make me feel uncomfortable, but she must have had to work really hard, especially considering that she'd had to raise Aoife alone in her early years.

With the awareness to note how impressed I was with her clear drive and ability to achieve what she'd set out to, despite the difficulties, Siobhan, as if reading my thoughts, mentioned, in a modest manner that she was lucky enough that her parents had been able to do a lot of the 'heavy lifting,' so to speak, early in Aoife's life. After those early years, when Aoife had got to about five years old, Siobhan had met her now husband and the two of them had been able to cope fairly comfortably together. They'd had another child after they were married, a brother for Aoife and young Dermot is now eleven years old.

While there's been an ease to many aspects of my life, I'd say there's also been lucklessness, multiple disappointments, let-downs, and, as such, I've trained myself with regards to expectations. I hadn't allowed myself to get my hopes up for a better life, a happier life in decades. But when Aoife messaged to say that her mum was visiting, I have to admit that I'd let myself dream a little, I'd let my mind gravitate towards wishful thinking and then onwards, entertaining the idea of possibility. Maybe love could blossom. It was foolish; they were thoughts detached, significantly detached, from what I knew to be the reality of this world, at least my world. They have been the outlandish wishes of a fairly desperate man. Sure, a man with a newly found bounce in his step, but desperate nevertheless.

I should have known, I did know really when I bothered to think logically, that Siobhan would've gone on to lead an interesting life, more interesting than the norm, and would attract a man better than I in the process. Sometimes you feel young in the presence of younger people, but for me to witness her, of similar age, so spritely and youthful, so switched on, with so much of her beauty intact, I felt old, worse even, as if I was older than my age. I used to get told that I was mature for my age when I was a teenager and, back then, I didn't entirely mind it, but now, to think yourself as older than you actually are, well, things have become different. It has been particularly noticeable to me that I'm overtly older-acting and looking than I should be, and, in response, I can't help but shift my thoughts towards self-reflection, self-criticism. I think it was obvious to all three of us that when we were in group conversation with Aoife, Siobhan was clearly so much younger in the mind than me in terms of the way she was able to connect with a different generation. She knew about all things that Aoife was talking about with regard to modern fashion and technology, while I stayed quiet for much of our conversations, hoping not to make it glaringly obvious that I had no idea what they would be talking about. I guess it is unsurprising that I don't know about these things as I have made, regrettably, no effort to keep up with the younger generation and have no natural link that having children or grandchildren likely gives you. I think though, regardless of our differences, I only struggled to converse on a superficial level and the same age-old problems that everyone has always had are still in existence, able to be shared and discussed. I remind myself in this way of my grandfather.

It was on the Saturday evening, after a glass of wine for Siobhan and a couple of beers for me at my local pub that we eventually got around to discussing the subject of us and how we used to be. We'd spent quite a bit of time in pubs during our brief relationship and there was a familiarity and comfort in sitting across from her, drink in hand. Aoife was with us as well, and it was her persistence in wanting to talk about how we'd met that, along with the wine, broke Siobhan's stubborn resistance to discussing the topic. Although there had been a gradual loosening of our inhibitions, her shyness and my tension, on the Friday night and during the day on the Saturday, I think it was only then that I started to reconnect properly with Siobhan. It made me feel great, and young dare I say, to reminisce. It is, quite naturally it seems, easier to remember the bad in life, so much so that when I recalled, we recalled, times of enjoyment it was so alien to me that it bordered on being thrilling. Incredibly, Siobhan had brought a photo of us that she'd kept all these years, perhaps a token reminder of me, hopefully reminding her of something good, and when she dug it out of her handbag it transported my mind back to when it was taken. It reminded me of days when I felt as though things just may be possible, not anything, just some things, that there was opportunity out there.

'What happened to us?' I said teasingly before quickly and quite rightly correcting myself. 'What happened to me?'

'I can still see the old spark in your eyes,' Siobhan responded. I think she might have been the only one. I permanently have sizable bags under my eyes these days that make me look like a close relation of a badger. A weak badger. 'Can you remember when this was taken?' Siobhan said.

'I think I do,' I responded affirmatively, 'that's Karl Marx' grave in Highgate Cemetery, isn't it?' It had been taken the morning before she'd left for Dublin and was something she'd wanted to see before leaving for home, for whatever reason I couldn't really identify with myself. An important historical figure, sure, but we'd had to get up at 6am to go there. I hadn't put up a fight against going, even though I was none too pleased about us spending our last morning together going on a sizable journey up to the far north of London. It was her want and so I'd gone along with it. I looked so alive, and dare I say, so happy in the photo that I was almost unrecognisable from what stares back at me in the mirror today. I was pulling a funny face for the photo, pointing my tongue towards Siobhan on my left as I lifted the point of my nose to look like a pig. A classic. I haven't goofed around for decades. I should've goofed around more. There was even a full, un-receding head of hair. Siobhan, for her part, looked enviously similar to how she is now and the spitting image of Aoife, or should I say Aoife is the spitting image of Siobhan in the photo. The feeling of how it was to be young flooded through me during the evening, how the excitement of a new relationship felt and we drank and laughed and even danced. It was the rarest of things, a night of fun, and it was one of the best nights of my life.

In what seemed like the blink of a beer induced bloodshot eye, Aoife and Siobhan were making their way through to departures at the same airport I'd picked them up from less than 72 hours earlier. Uncharacteristically, before they left, and while it embarrassed me slightly to do so, I felt compelled to impart some of what little wisdom I may have on Aoife. In our two encounters I've learnt a lot, acknowledging that although I haven't lived a particularly active life, I have my own experience of an uneventful yet eventful life, and that has given me a degree of wisdom gained, albeit, through nothing more than living for a decent length of time.

No doubt, the wording was poor and my speech stilted, but I think I got my message across. I'm unsure as to why entirely, but I found myself overcome with emotion as I was speaking and, as my heart rate increased and my face got redder, a tear fell down my cheek. What a strange old man. How embarrassing. I told her I was glad that she has a loving family, including her dad, and that I was an example of what not to do in life. My message was to learn from my mistake, that even if she was uncertain of whether a choice will make her happy there are no certainties in life, no way to know, and that she should go for it anyway, should cling to it, any possibility of happiness, and even if it turns out to go horribly wrong she would not regret trying.

'I let life pass me by, and I retreated from new people, new things, and new opportunities because I had fear. Whatever happens, be braver than me. It's the decision you don't make, the things you don't try, the journeys you don't make that you will regret. It's the words you didn't say.' I paused before saying something quite unexpected. 'I love you Aofie, you might be my only achievement in this life.' She stared at me, not knowing what to say, and hugged me tightly. She whispered that it's not too late to try new things and that she would see me again. A tear fell down her cheek as well. She's perfect.

15

It's been a long while since my last entry. After Aoife and Siobhan's departure I settled, quite naturally, into a state of familiar melancholy. The blues I guess you could call it. I was sluggish in my mind and at no point particularly enthused by the idea of getting out of bed. The memory of our weekend together has begun to fade and without reading that past chapter to myself, I would struggle to recall the details of it. As has become common, I'm left with the memory of the way the weekend made me feel without being able to remember why I felt that way, my memories relegated from the specifics of the short-term memory to a general feeling of warmth and happiness in the long.

While it's hard to know what can be, should be, classed as success in life, I'd say that Siobhan has made a success of hers. She seemed happy; I guess that's the key point, with a solid marriage, a great daughter, a body that wasn't failing her and a good income. As such, she's been able to provide Aoife with a level of security in her life that anybody would wish their children to have. It's strange to think that I could be so deeply affected by the departure of Aoife, somebody that I've met just twice and didn't know existed for twenty years. It's my expectation, one I've developed as I've gotten to know her a little bit, that, unlike me, she won't waste the opportunity that her parents, not me, have given her. She will, and should, take after her mother rather than me, and I have little doubt that she'll do something worthwhile with her life, probably helping people in some way. And if she ever has children of her own she will no doubt provide them with the same security that her parents provided her and my parents provided for me.

Thinking about what parents can provide their children prompted me to visit the graves of mine yesterday, buried next to one another in a coastal cemetery, overlooking a sheltered bay to the south of the island. I placed some flowers in remembrance and, as I've done many times over the last few months, sat, reflected, and actually thought about them, what they were like, what I recall, not to grieve but to remember and to be thankful, thinking. There is a bench there, looking out to sea, a spot I've become fond of, sometimes sitting for hours on end depending on the weather of the day, contemplating, reflecting. I placed some tulips on the ground above my dear old mum's grave, purple and white, fresh. Purple tulips were mum's favourite, and seeing them and smelling them would improve her mood, right up to the end of her life.

At the flower shop, on the way to the cemetery, I'd run into somebody who I'd met the day before when out for a walk on the beach. Only, concerningly, I couldn't recall meeting them the day before. I'd stopped at a small kiosk there, on the windswept, empty beach to have a cup of tea when a man had, so he says, struck up a conversation with me. I remember the walk on the beach but this man, burly, barrel-chested and bald recognised me at the flower shop and mentioned how nice it had been on the beach the day before.

'Fresh,' he said. I nodded and said,

'Oh yes, I sometimes find that weather to be the best,' maintaining for once, I think, nonchalance. I had no recollection of our encounter and my fakery reminded me of how my mother would pretend to recall events of which she had no recollection. I tried to forget about it, ironically, and I'm taking solace in the fact that I'm not able to do so. I remember the conversation at the florist, and while it's possible that he was mistaken about our encounter, I find it concerning that at my age I may be getting forgetful.

My body is beginning to fail me, no doubt, not in a serious manner but I have increasing aches and pains, particularly in the morning around my lower back. Those things I can deal with but, having witnessed what happened to my dear old mum, I hope, possibly even pray, that my mind can remain sharp. The truth is though prayers might be a desperate requirement due to some worrying signs. There have been small things, like failing to remember where I've parked the car, as with Siobhan and Aoife, where I've left my car keys, a classic but of increasing frequency, and whether or not, like my mum used to do, I've already put sugar in my tea. Indeed, I had a cuppa the other day that tasted as if it had at least three hefty spoonfuls of sugar in. I laughed it off just like she used to.

It's not just the random acts or none acts of forgetfulness that are problematic. When I write now, my ability to conjure words, the appropriate words from my mind has become notably more difficult. While the art of conversing has always been problematic ever since I was young, I've been reasonably good with writing, able to spell and remember the meanings of complicated words, excelling, to a certain degree, in primary school spelling tests. Always hold on to success, it's rare. But, on occasion now, I'm really struggling to recall and spell words and create sentences, sometimes even simple ones. It's as if they are there, in my mind, but I have to concentrate, sometimes quite a bit harder than normal to access them. Writing anything, close to being of a reasonable standard, takes me an alarmingly long time these days, and while I hope it's an everyday brand of ageing, I'm struggling more at night to recall things, just as my dear old mum did in the beginning. Mimicking her further, I find too that I have a propensity to get abnormally frustrated and angry with myself when these failures of memory occur. I have been telling myself to stay calm, so often my default setting, so often so natural, but it's as if I'm slowly falling apart. I'm falling apart right in front of my own eyes and there's seemingly nothing I can do about the situation. To try and stay calm in such circumstances is near impossible, even for a person like me. I'm anxious.

The central issue driving my anxiety is the inevitability of the one-way direction on the path once I start going down it, the slow march towards nothingness. If I'm identifying it now I'm probably already going down it. Even if things like brain tumours or types of cancer can be scary, because of the magnitude of the problem, you do hear stories about recovery and survival, and living healthy lives thereafter. There is often a degree of hope there. I don't think, however, that I've ever heard about anybody getting better when things start to fade in the mind. For all the time that I sat and watched my mother, for the time that I saw her lack of recognition destroy my dear old dad, I never thought perhaps, never wanted to think that it would, could, happen to me. I've written, often joking of my physical deterioration that's openly been on display in recent years, never wanting to contemplate that rather than my heart or liver it's my brain that may be the organ to fail me first.

My occasional newly found worry induced anger aside and the most prevalent feelings I have at the moment when thinking the end of the road might be nigh are embarrassment and foolishness, born out of the knowledge that I never tried harder in life. I never went after the A grade, I never tried to climb the mountain (literally and figuratively), and I never really chased *the girl,* or even let her know how I felt. Not as I should have anyway. If I press myself now for a reason as to why I was so passive, if I genuinely consider it rather than avoiding asking myself an unpleasant question, I can't think of one reasonable explanation for my inactive nature. I guess that I've always thought there would be another chance, another opportunity to do what I could be doing now. Always. I told myself this life, which I've always known, especially since the death of Sam, doesn't last that long, would still provide me with enough time in the future to be able to do what I should be doing today. It turns out that it wasn't and it doesn't.

To like the person I am, I was, is difficult. To be comfortable with the person I have come to understand the importance of understanding what shaped me, what made me how I am, who I am. Yet, I have to reconcile that with the fact that I myself had choices, I had my own agency over my decisions. My own personality, as much as it has been manufactured by the environment around me, and the things in life that have happened to me, I still had control of the decisions I've made. My lack of activity, my reclusiveness, as much as it may have been brought on me, was still a path I chose. I chose not to fight, not to get through it, not to push through to the other side. I chose to let it fester, to eat away at me, to inform my decision-making. I took the easy option to wallow in fear and self-pity after Chantelle, after Sam, and I chose to do the bare minimum with the privilege afforded to me by the island, by my hard-working parents. I've hidden myself and now, now I can see the end, I'm not sure why.

I will go and get myself tested to see what is going on, but when I search my own mind for the truth, I know that this is the beginning of the end.

16

Maybe it'll become easier; maybe this is the hardest part. I went to the doctor, took some tests, physical, mental, mainly mental, and I've recently been diagnosed with the disease. The testing reminded me a lot of when I'm writing, that frustration-inducing inability to access information in my head that I felt I should be able to access without thought. Indeed, I've arrived at a stage now where I understand what is happening to me, still understand, and that's why I wonder whether it'll become easier. I am depressed, irritable and angry, and while I'm conscious of what is happening to me and try to maintain a degree of positivity, these are my default emotions, impossible to deny and difficult to control. I punched a wall last week in response to being unable to locate my coat and then finding it, before failing to remember why I needed it in the first place. I followed the outburst of anger with a hysterical laughter, half hyena, half sea lion, dropping to the floor and lying on my back on the worn beige carpet in the lounge.

This is the torturous part that I saw in my dear old mum; a period of time when a person has the awareness that they are forgetting things and yet know worse is to come. I'm losing any sense of what I was, knowing there's no point of return, only taking a small amount of solace in the fact that maybe, at some point, probably quite soon, I'll just forget that

I'm forgetting, and all the anxiety, all the frustrations, will likely fall away as my faulty mind decays irreparably.

What with the relative certainty of me deteriorating into a near vegetative state as time elapses, there is another option, the drastic option. During my dear old mother's illness I don't think I was ever able to empathise with the level of fear she must've been feeling, particularly in the early stages, this stage I'm in, with the awareness of what was happening. I think back to the jokes that she would make about being forgetful that we, initially at least, encouraged and made ourselves, me and my dad, and recognise it now as our family coping mechanism. It doesn't seem at all funny now, and while Mum did at least have my dear old dad, and to a lesser extent me to help her through it, I'm very much alone in this and not wanting to burden anybody else, I won't be seeking help. I guess you can never really truly understand somebody else's experience in anything until you experience the same thing, or something similar. Chantelle knew that.

It is tempting to end it all, particularly if I become a burden to others, and who knows what I will feel in the coming weeks and months, but for now, as long as I feel like there is a semblance of me, a semblance of normality I may as well keep going. If I can still read, write and speak, however difficult and stilted it might be, I feel as though I'd like to keep living, going for autumn walks, watching the leaves fall, looking out to an angry sea or smelling the flowers in spring-time bloom in my garden. As soon as I'm unable to take pleasure in those things, I'd like for it to all be over. The catch in that logic is that I'm unlikely to be of sound mind by that point to do anything about it, even if I'd have the capability or will to do so. It's curious, perhaps, that I've spent many weeks and months in my life unwilling and unable to get out of bed, feeling largely indifferent to the idea of being alive, and now, now that I know it's all coming to a head, I just wish I had a little more time.

Words. Sure, finding the right ones is something that I've always struggled with when in conversation, especially important ones, but it has never been, it *had* never been, so much of an issue with the pen in hand. I need that relaxation, a sense of calm in my mind in order to be able to write anything good or bad, and finally, only now have I been able to get the right conditions. Recently, I've been preparing for the end, getting my 'affairs in order,' and only today has that quite drawn out and anxiety inducing process come to an end. It has given me great peace of mind to have it done. As each prior day had passed I'd become increasingly concerned, in my newly acquired frantic nature, that I would not have it finished before my mind entirely deserted me. But it's done. I have left, or rather will be leaving, everything I have to Aoife.

Sure, with no kids of my own and no nephews or nieces, Aoife is really the only choice for me to leave everything to, but I'm happy, extremely happy to leave my lot to her. Having gotten to know her, albeit only over a few days, I'm wholly confident that she is a wonderful and responsible person, which gives me a solid comfort in the knowledge that leaving what I have to her is a sound decision. It's true that she already has had a life of relative privilege, and this will only add to it, but I'm convinced that, unlike me, she will use that advantage to do something meaningful, either to live an extraordinarily adventurous life herself, or to help those not provided with the same level of security and opportunity, or both. I have no doubt that she understands her privilege and the further privilege this inheritance will give to her, and for that reason I have no qualms with providing her with my wealth.

Indeed, I recently received a letter from Aoife, a good old letter! If my decision was not already decided, that certainly did it. She let me know how well she's getting on at university and expressed to me how much she was looking forward to visiting me again. In fact, she implored me to get off the island and go to the UK to see her. When we first met, and then when her mum visited, it was true that I felt a sense of rejuvenation in my life, a compulsion to come out from my secure slumber, to do something adventurous, or at least relatively adventurous, but now unfortunately, I've had to admit to myself that I'm unable to do so. I have deteriorated too much mentally, and there is the chance that in unfamiliar surroundings, I would forget where I was or why I was there, and that is terrifying to me. I'm also frightened, frankly, and would be embarrassed to let her see me like this, all flustered and forgetful. I sent her a letter back, making my excuses. 'The body isn't what it was,' etc. It has pained me to do so because I would have loved to have visited her, but I can't let her see me like this.

For many many years, too many years, years when I had the option to do so, I never had the inclination to leave the island. I always had options. And now, now that I understand there will be no more firsts, I truly feel vulnerable to the elapsing of time. There is little left for me, what I have done will be all that I have done and that is likely to soon extend to this book. There are unlikely to be many, or any, new entries in this book as I have an increasing inability to recall recent events, at least not in any detail. Indeed, not only am I unlikely to be able to do new things, I am even less likely to be able to recall them at all, even fast becoming unable to recall stories about me being unable to remember things.

My Uncle Peter, the unreliable one who had joked about looking after me, died when I was relatively young. I was in my early twenties at the time, and, to be honest, I thought very little of it. Just one of those things, part of it all. But what I do recall is the way people spoke about his illness. He was a builder by trade and was a suitably well-built man, tall and strong with a wide jaw and gigantic, rough hands. He died due to a tumor, some sort of cancer, pancreatic I think, and during his end months his ordeal was described by friends and family as a fight. The language people used, my dear old mum included, made it seem as though it was a battle against an advancing enemy, as if a battle was there to be won, the enemy could be put on the retreat, and victory in the war was possible. Evidently, in Peter's case, the enemy, the invading force, grew too strong and the war was lost, but I recall the sense that victory was attainable. What I have doesn't feel like that, I'd say it's something entirely different. There is a sense that survival is possible against an enemy that is visible. For this, for me, it's as though I keep getting robbed by a thief who is impossible to see and impossible to stop. Eventually, all of my possessions will disappear without me knowing how they've been taken or where they've gone. Or possibly that they're missing at all. A few bits have gone already and now more and more are disappearing. I know the thief will return, frequently, and I know there is nothing I can do. I am helpless.

That helplessness is what's left; it's the foundation for all of my other emotions. The fear, the anger, even the occasional flicker of bravery, it all stems from an understanding that I have no control over anything. My motor skills have receded and getting dressed is now an extremely strenuous task, buttoning, unbuttoning, and my handwriting, never tidy at the best of times, has deteriorated considerably as I fail to write straight on lined paper. I have good days and bad days, good hours and bad hours, and while I'm in a good place right now with a degree of self-awareness and a clarity of thought, I know it's temporary and that the muddled darkness will return and it will last longer every time it returns.

17

A pretty young girl knocked on my door just now and I've decided to quickly write down the moment. I felt like I should have recognised her and it seemed as though she expected me to. I was agitated on her arrival, quite naturally, but she soon put me at ease with her general manner. She seemed nice and I think she's going to help me; maybe she'll even help with the book.

ABOUT THE AUTHOR

Entirely hairless and gender sideways, Kaspar Zeitgeist is the thirteenth child of the eighty-seventh high-priestess of the ancient Queendom of Baloneya, the greatest queendom to never exist.

Literally spineless, held together by wooden splints and a single sticky tape, Zeitgeist strongly dislikes adventure, preferring monotony, familiarity, and a dull shade of grey known as milky carbon only found on the walls of his living quarters.

This fondness for nothing means Zeitgeist detests any political system involving change and choice, instead favouring the stability provided by the constant rule of a single figure, alive, dead, or robot, with unwavering and uncompromising views on all stuff.

Printed in Great Britain
by Amazon